Hey, This is it, I'm Going to Die

Short Stories
by
Ron Heacock

LIBROS IGNI
www.libros-igni.com

FIRST LIBROS IGNI EDITION, NOVEMBER 2014

Published by Libros Igni, Portland, OR
www.libros-igni.com

ISBN 0-9909387-0-0

Several of the stories in this collection were previously published. "Sharp's Rifle" was previously published in *PaperTape Magazine* under the title of "The Gun". "Where They Go" appeared in *Connotation Press*. "The Sand is White in Jamaica" appeared in *Far Enough East*. "A Day in the Life" was published by *The Rejected Writer*. "Badger Will Lead You Home" appeared in Elohi Gadugi Journal. "Some Demons Don't Die" was published in *The Gambler*. "Hey, This is it, I'm Going to Die" was previously published in *Cease Cows* under the name "Inarguably Dead". "Marsha Griggs" was included in a special Halloween issue of *LIMN Literary Arts Journal*. "Abraham's Absolution" appeared in *Under the Influence of Words*.

I will never be able to thank all the people who helped with these stories. I would not be here at all without my parents, and I am sorry that they didn't live to see this accomplishment. My wife Karen Walasek has always been my partner, muse, and guide. I thank my children, Justin, Morgan, Galen, and Steve for understanding my insanity. Thank you for supporting for my art: Burt Heacock and Theresa Ostrowski, Jessica and Michael Poulin, and all of my immediate and not so immediate family. This work would not have been written without Goddard College, my undergraduate cohort, and advisors. Specifically, I need to thank Robert Braile, Ryan Boudinot, Walter Butts, and Newcomb Greenleaf. Special thanks and gratitude for ideas and encouragement are owed to Josh Amses, Ed Atkinson, David Bernbaum, Drew Lundgren, Kate Roberts, and Lisa Wells. Molto grazie to Libros Igni, Gorham Printing, and Alison Bailey for midwifing this project.

If I forgot to mention anyone, please forgive the oversight.

Contents

for Karen, my one and only love

Sharp's Rifle

I did not ask for the gun, but I am honored to have received it. The dogs knew the boy was there before I did and although they tried to warn me, I could not understand. You see, like most rural residents, my dogs are my alarm system. Of course they create a ruckus over almost any disturbance; it doesn't have to be a threat. The Little One doesn't see very well and, for some mysterious reason, the others think that she is some kind of early warning system. She hears a pipe ping or catches the shadow of a fluttering leaf and it's a four alarm fire. The other two idiots just react and amplify.

There is a different kind of barking that they indulge in now and again. That's when a usurper has crossed into their domain. Traditionally it is another dog. People in my county know better than to wander uninvited onto someone else's land. You might get yourself shot. When the dogs detect a trespasser they go berserk, like a motion detector has been tripped; some faint seismic activity, invisible and silent to my dull senses, causes repeated alerts at all hours.

That night they started in around midnight. Now, at my age, I don't normally sleep more than a few hours, but they were ringing the bell every hour on the hour, so by dawn I realized I had not been sleeping at all.

In late June the sun comes up before five and even though I had no reason to be up that early, the sun was a welcome excuse to *get up already and let the damn dogs out*. Usually the lazy mutts will not even come downstairs when I go to make the coffee, but they were whining and door-scratching. I figured there was a stray sniffing around the chickens.

Being stiff and sleepy, I shuffled down the stairs and opened the front door without even looking. "Git-em," I mumbled, as they exploded outside, a howling dog tornado. Before I could even get the door latched I heard a ferocious "BANG" and a yip.

It's funny how some sounds can just rattle the sleepiness right out of you. I was awake and in the front lawn before I knew how I'd gotten there wearing nothing but a pair of boxers and torn cotton T shirt. The dogs had scattered. Finn and Little One were on the porch already, dazed and panting. The terrier, Loki, was nowhere to be seen. I rounded the corner of the house to confront the source of the noise and caught sight of what appeared to be a teen-aged boy dressed in an ill-fitting Yankee civil war re-enactment costume. He was fumbling the breach open, apparently attempting to reload a long barreled rifle. Without thinking I called out, "Hey, what the hell..."

He snapped around to face me, bringing the firearm up, its bayonet glinting in the early morning sun. I raised my hands over my head and yelled across the yard to him: "There's no need for that son. Put down the gun and let's see what this is about."

His image seemed to waver in the rising heat. He did not lower the gun. I was suddenly overwhelmed by the intensity of the colors; the green of the covering sugar maples and the lushness of the grass; every blade and leaf stood out separate and vibrating slightly. The rust-red barn behind him and the black wood fence running up to the forest-green tube gate were almost glowing. The sky, an unusual shade of ultramarine, was streaked with tattered wisps of silver.

And then there was his uniform. It was the deepest navy blue and the jacket buttons were bright gold. Funny thing I realized later is that there was no heat; the wavering must have been something else, because I didn't imagine it. The image is burned in my memory as clear as a high-resolution photo: green grass, blue boy, red barn.

I was pretty sure he hadn't had time to reload and, standing a hundred paces in front of me, the bayonet posed little threat. It crossed my mind that if he decided to charge I would look pretty ridiculous, an old man, sprinting through the lawn in my underwear. The thought made me smile. I guess it smoothed my voice out when I said, "Son, you don't want to hurt no one. Lower your weapon and let's you and me have a talk."

You know, I couldn't really see his face at that distance. Just the same, I could swear that I saw the tears in his eyes before I heard the sob. He fell to his knees. The bayonet point stuck into the lawn as he bent forward and pressed his face into his hands.

I will always be a father no matter that my children have long ago moved away from home. And that young soldier, even though he was only dressed up as one, crying before me touched a deep place in my heart.

I walked over and knelt beside him. He looked directly into my eyes and said, "I'm not a man who kills widows and babies. She looked like my sister. I will never wash the blood from my hands. Look." He held his dirty palms up to my face. I did not see any blood. "It has stained them permanent and I will be damned to hell forever for what I have done."

He just fell over before I could speak. I didn't know if he was asleep or unconscious. Loki had showed up and he licked at his face. The boy mumbled, "Mercy, please." At least he wasn't dead.

I couldn't leave him out there on the grass, but I had no intention of dragging him into the house. I started up to the porch and turned around thinking, "It might be best if I just put that gun inside for him while I go about getting dressed." I called Loki, but he wouldn't budge. He'd hunkered down in the grass next to the boy. I figured that it had been a while since he had a young man around. Kids go off and leave their childhoods at home along with their childhood pets. I went inside and dressed, filled a glass with cool water from the fridge and brought it back outside.

When I stepped off the porch the shimmering around the boy's body had intensified and the colors were brighter still. The landscape behind him changed as I watched. I heard a strange out-of-phase wind blowing. I do not know exactly how to describe the sound of it. The subtle blanket of the morning birds slid between forefront and background with a clanking rumble of voices, animals and harnesses.

Smoke drifted from somewhere nearby. The fences of my front field evaporated and, replacing the rolling pasture, normally dotted with cattle, was the most astonishing panorama I have ever witnessed. This was no civil war re-enactment. This was real. A sprawling army of men and tents, horses and wagons, cannon and low lying smoke covered the scorched battlefield that now ran from where Pigeon Roost Road should have been, across Sneed's thousand acres to the woods beyond. I shook my head to try and clear it. In response, the scene became more vivid, crystallizing. A pair of uniformed men supporting the boy on their shoulders led him away and down the incline toward the heart of the encampment. He forgot his hat and damp hair hung limp across his face, his head lolled from side to side as they half-dragged, half-walked him away. I distinctly heard him repeat: "Mercy, please," and one of the others answered, "We need all the mercy we can get, William. Come on now, you'll be better soon."

9

Loki trotted along at his heel, looking up at him as though he had a rare steak in his pocket. I thought to call after him but I didn't. In truth I couldn't speak. My throat had closed up and tears were blurring my vision. I blinked hard to clear my eyes and wiped at my face with the back of my hand. The smoke was acrid and greasy, the sky over the encampment purple and bruised. All the earth surrounding them was pitted with cannon craters and several trees were splintered and burning.

My horror grew the longer I watched. My ears were filled with men's screams and the shrill whinnying of horses. Every so often a loud gunshot punctuated the background murmuring of this writhing city.

I could take no more.

I turned away and looked past my back yard to the rolling hills dotted with round bales fresh from the first cutting. I suddenly realized that I still had the boy's gun. Without turning to look at the army on the front fields, I went into the house and grabbed the rifle. I did not consider how I would explain myself: a Southern man in a Northern encampment. My only concern was returning the weapon to a soldier who would need it.

When I stepped off the staircase into the yard the entire bivouac had vanished. It took a long moment to realize my mouth was open. I closed it, scanning the fields again for a sign of the army that I had just witnessed. The smell of all that death and smoke still filled my nose, but the sky was clear and a cow lowed in the distance. As I crossed the dirt driveway, walking toward my front fence, my toe caught on something sticking out of the soil. With the gun in my hand and I bent down and pried a Federal army crossed-cannon emblem from the soil. A little scratching around unearthed an engraved name plate and two brass hat buttons.

Loki never returned. I guess that boy needed him more than he needed me.

The gun is an 1861 Sharps, 54 caliber falling block action three-band rifle; it has only been fired a few times. There is a pellet primer still in it and an unfired brass-cased round. Presumably, William actually got it loaded, intending to shoot the dogs or me. Its existence is impossible. You see, aside from the proper patent engravings and the serial number, which falls in the range of the Berdan Sharpshooter rifles, the iron it was forged from is very unique. It was founded from ore mined in northeastern Massachusetts. It has a specific spectrographic signature. This ore ran out in 1870. But the gun that I took from William, as well as the primer cap and bullet, are new. They show no sign of age and no wear from use. It is as if the gun and cartridge were made a few years ago. There were only 500 of these fire arms ever made.

After considerable expert wrangling, the gun was pronounced an authentic civil war artifact and appraised at 1.5 million dollars. I will leave it to my children. I cannot bring myself to sell it regardless of my need and its value.

As final note you should know that boy was William Heacock. His name was engraved on the plate that came from his hat and his initials were carved into the burl walnut buttstock of his rifle. His family lived in Bucks County Pennsylvania. He had a sister and four brothers of whom all but one died on the battlefield across from my farm in 1864. The one surviving son was named Emerson Heacock and he was my great grandfather. I have never told anyone where I got that gun until today.

Where They Go

"Mom, where do they go when they die?"

She was loading bags of groceries into the trunk of the car. She did not answer. I walked over to the bird lying on the brown mulch piled up next to a skinny tree. The mulch was surrounded by a concrete curb in the FoodMart parking lot. The bird, one dull beady eye staring, was some kind of brown and grey sparrow-like thing. One wing was stretched out and its neck bent the wrong way.

"Mom?" I repeated, looking down at the bird.

She must have thought I was going to pick it up because she grabbed my shoulder and pulled me toward the car. I might have already bent down. The sun glinted off the chrome bumper.

"Don't touch dead birds, Sammy, they carry diseases."

"Where do they carry them?" I asked.

She didn't answer, just pushed me into the back seat and closed the car door. I could hear her through the rolled up windows, "You didn't touch it did you? Buckle up now, you know, seat belts save lives."

ஐ

"It's a sin to tell a lie," she said.

It was a different day and the weather was cooler. We were in the garage, having just returned from the eye doctor. After she closed the garage door the sun shined through the cracks between the door panels, painting lines on the cement floor. It smelled like fertilizer, motor oil, and gasoline. I told her that I dreamed I was in the backyard, but then I woke up, and I really *was* in the backyard. The grass was wet. I was in my pajamas looking up at the cold, black, starry sky. I started to cry, and I wished I were back in my bed. So that's why there were leaves and stuff on the sheets this morning; 'Cause my feet got dirty in a dream.

I asked, "What's a sin?"

The water is freezing. The bathroom has blue tiles on the walls and the tub is blue too, just lighter. They must have filled it with ice cubes and then they put me in. My skin burns all over my whole body. My hands and feet feel huge. I am fighting with strong hands. Everything in the room is tilted and wrong: The toilet looks too big and the shower curtain around my dad's face looks tiny. He is speaking, but I can't understand the words. I can see up his nose, smell the cigarettes on his breath. I wonder: Why are you killing me? I am crying, pleading for my mommy. "Mommy, get me out!" I was so cold before, and now I am on fire. When I close my eyes everything is orange with yellow at the edges. I want to be out of the water, but I am confused and afraid. As I gasp for air, I hear someone say, "Shush, it's okay," and then the little tiled room fills with screams again. The screams come from me.

I am sitting on my grandfather's rocking chair on his porch somewhere far away from home. My feet do not touch the floorboards where the grey paint is peeling. It is summer, and flies are flying around the dirty rug in front of the screen door where Chester, my grandpa's dog, sleeps. It smells hot and dirty like old cooking grease.

Chester is mean. I have been bitten, but he is nowhere around now. I want a Good Humor. I want to be home watching cartoons. I want to be anywhere but here. The flies land on me, in my face, on my hands. My mom has warned me about the germs. I am afraid to touch the grimy railing or the grimy doorknob. I squeeze my eyes shut. I remember Dorothy in the movie *The Wizard of OZ*. I whisper, "There's no place like home, there's no place like home." I hold my breath; I strain and push and grit my teeth. Sweat runs down my forehead, into my eyes. It tickles my nose; I wipe at it with the side of my hand.

When I open my eyes I am still here. The air is so hot and still that the fence in the front yard looks like it is a reflection in the lake. I remember the lake. The water is cold and dark and deep. I think about the splintery wood on the dock, the metal boat tied up with a thick, scratchy, knotted rope, a black tire tube floating. I can hear the little waves splashing against the posts and the boat banging against the dock.

I no longer want to go anywhere. The idea of the lakeside is just like being there. I relax. I hear other kids playing nearby. When I open my eyes I am sitting on the little sandy beach by the water. A motor boat skims by out in the middle of the lake.

She is old. We have had her ever since I can remember. I put my face into the wiry brown fur on her heaving side and listen to her insides: Breathing, panting. Like a city of noises gurgling underground. Shallow breaths, up and down—in and out.

They tell me she is dying. I know that it means she will go away. Somewhere.

I ask, "Why?" There is no answer. I ask, "Where will Brownie go?"

My dad walks away. My mom says, "Heaven, dear, she is going to heaven."

I have heard this before. I know they don't know where that is.

I lean in near her ear. It is very soft. She is panting little pants. I say, "It's okay now, you can go." Her tail lifts and falls once, twice. The muscles in her shoulder tighten, and her head lifts off the floor just a little. I think for a moment that she is going to get up, and I move away to give her some space. But she drops back onto the floor and sighs a long whistling exhale. The panting stops. Her eye is closed, like she is asleep, but I know she isn't. She's gone. Brownie's body is there but not Brownie. I think: I wonder where she is.

Wallstone's Black Duchess. She was the one. I could just tell. One in a jumble of black, tan, and white fur; wobbling on unsteady legs. It was hard to imagine that this little fuzzy rat would someday grow into a dog. Her brothers and sisters squeaked and growled, tumbling over one another in the open cardboard box.

Mom said, "She will be bigger than Brownie, you know. Collies are big, athletic dogs. You are going to have to walk her every day."

I was hardly listening. I held the little puffball with my thumbs hooked under her front legs and raised the tiny black nose to mine. Her puppy eyes were still blue, sort-of unfocused.

My dad said, "I think we're going to take this one. Sammy? You can call her Duchess."

The puppy stopped squirming. Her hind legs hung limp. Her little pink tongue flicked out and kissed me. I thought: Is that you?

I said, "Mom? I think she recognizes me. It's Brownie! She's come back home to me."

My sixth period math teacher, Mr. Mulligan, was the most boring man on the planet. If I wasn't drawing a battle between the Cylons and the Federation on the inside cover of my math notebook, I would have been asleep. While Mulligan droned on about multiplying negative fractions, I saw the janitor, Joe Stern, out the window, riding around and around in circles on the Columbia Middle School lawn mower.

I thought he had to be getting dizzy, just going in circles like that. Mulligan's voice, the low humming of the motor through the closed windows, and the hot room became too much. I watched a fly land on the windowsill and crawl around, buzzing on and off. Outside, Mr. Stern went around and around and around. My eyes began to close.

I must have fallen asleep, because when the breeze hit my face, I woke up standing in the fresh cut grass outside. The janitor turned just in time to avoid running me over. I stood there blinking. I didn't know how I got there. I told them, but they didn't believe me. I got three days of detention for leaving the building without a pass.

By the time I was in high school, it had happened enough times that I realized I might end up wherever my attention focused. I was jumpy and nervous, worrying that it would happen unexpectedly. My grades were horrible and I wasn't sleeping.

I met Alice in the cafeteria. She sat next to me and said, "I remember you from middle school. I was in Mulligan's class that day, and I saw you disappear." We became pretty good friends. She told me, "You have a gift, Sammy; you should practice it to make it stronger, like a muscle." She wanted to help.

My mom had gone back to work, so there was nobody to bother us at my house. Alice suggested I try simple moves at first, like from the den to the bathroom. I discovered that all I had to do was to clearly imagine one detail, like the pattern in the counter top or the way the chrome around the sink drain was chipped, and I would find myself sitting on the toilet or on the edge of the bathtub. A moment later Alice would call after me: "Hey Sammy, you in there?"

I wanted to teach her how I did it, but she didn't want to try. Once I grabbed her hand just before I *moved*, but she yanked it back and stormed out of the house. We never talked about it, and I didn't bring it up again. Alice was my only friend.

One afternoon just before Christmas my mom and dad showed up at school together. I was called down to the office; they told me to go by my locker and collect my stuff. We drove all night to a hospital in Saint Louis. My grandpa was very ill, and he might not live through the night. When we arrived in the morning the priest was just leaving. My grandpa was a big, gruff man; I used to be afraid of him. But he looked small and pale in that hospital bed. His color reminded me of an old shirt that has been washed too many times.

My mom said, "Dad? Sammy's here, and Paul... We're all here to say goodbye, Dad. Can you hear me?" She motioned for me to come closer.

I really wanted to get away from that room. If I let myself, I could be somewhere else in a moment, but it would be hard to explain. I moved up next to him, and he mumbled. I asked, "What did you say grandpa?"

I sat down in the chair next to the bed. My mom said, "Listen Sam, you stay here with him for a bit. Your dad and I are going for coffee. Do you want anything?" I shook my head.

I sat there listening to his breathing. He had those little tubes under his nose, and he would wheeze on every exhale. I looked around the room. There was a plastic bed pan, a vase of wilting flowers, the TV remote. It seemed so sad and superficial that my big strong grandfather was dying in such a cruddy little room.

He suddenly opened his eyes, but he wasn't looking at me. He said, very clearly, "I don't know how to do this."

"Do what grandpa?"

"I can't find it. I can't find the door..."

I thought of the time in the ice bath. My mom told me that I had a 106-degree fever, and they were afraid I was going to die. It gave me an idea, I said, "Can you see an orange light, grandpa?"

"Where's the light? I can't find the light." He was only taking short, little breaths.

I imagined the pulsing orange light with the yellow around the edges. I looked into the image in my mind and noticed that it was like a flame. Little blue sparks shot out of the center like ribbons. I was standing in front of an open doorway with the orange light radiating from the room on the other side. It wasn't hot or anything. My grandpa was standing next to me looking off to the side. I took his big, soft hand, and pulled him forward. I said, "Look Gramps, there's the door, you want to go through it? It's okay you know. I think that's where you're supposed to go."

He didn't look at me. He said "Oh yes." Then he walked through and disappeared into the light.

I watched for a moment; my heart was pounding, but not because I was scared. I wondered where he was going, and I wanted to follow, but I remembered my mom and dad. The next moment I was sitting in the chair. I looked over at the body on the bed. A faint smile curled the corner of his ashen lips, but my grandfather was already gone.

❧❦

The Sand is White in Jamaica

"I don't belong in my body. I've always felt clumsy and disconnected, you know?"

Tynor, a shock of blond hair spilling into his eyes, munched a large organic carrot as he spoke. He gestured with it as though it were a fat, orange conductor's baton. He continued, "My hands feel just like two balloons, man. Sometimes anyway." He sighed. "You dig?" He wrenched a soaring power chord out of his air guitar, the carrot transformed into a pick or a paddle or a fly swatter. He snapped another bite off, nodding and smiling broadly as he chewed. The sixteen-year-old boy looked like some sort of demented jazz man in his wrap-around shades and black beret. He sat there bopping along to music only he could hear.

Dr. Warren scribbled on a yellow legal pad with his Pilot razor-point. He recognized his patient's reference to the Pink Floyd anthem *Comfortably Numb*, and asked, "Do you identify with the character, Pink, in the film *The Wall*, Tynor?

"Oh *def*-initly Doc. It takes all of my self-control to keep from snapping a double-edged razor blade in half and scrapping my eye brows off into the bathroom sink every morning!"

Tynor continued banging away at the imaginary guitar. He thought, I could probably pull my dick out of my pants and Pete wouldn't even blink. Maybe I should try it.

Dr. Peter Warren, Ph.D. – a psychologist – drew doodles in the margin. He made the agreement sound, "Hmmmm," but his mind drifted. He wondered what Selma was cooking for dinner. He could smell something cooking in the kitchen adjacent to his home office. He wondered: How could a man with three advanced degrees have married a woman who can't cook?

It was going to be the Yankee pot roast again. Selma thought he liked the Yankee pot roast, but the greasy meat, over-cooked carrots and potatoes gagged him. Now all he could think about was that damned pot roast. He wanted to tell Tynor to lose the carrot, but instead he glanced at his watch, not really seeing the time.

"Our time is just about up here, Tynor. Before we close for to-day, have you had any more, ah, episodes?" He pushed his reading glasses up off the tip of his nose with the end of the pen and tried to make eye contact with his patient.

Tynor thought, Oh Christ, I've gotta get away from this asshole!

To Dr. Warren, Tynor seemed lost in his own world. He couldn't tell if the boy's eyes were open or shut.

"Tynor, do you have any more to tell me? Okay, then, we'll see you next Tuesday." He pushed the rolling chair back from his desk and prepared to stand, glancing at his pad. It was mostly blank with a few mazes drawn in the margins. When he looked up the boy was gone.

Dr. Warren looked at his watch again. He stepped to the window in the door which led outside; no sign of Tynor. He removed his glasses and dropped them into his shirt pocket, pushing the curtains back from the edge of the glass and looking the other way. Nope, Tynor had simply vanished.

"I must be losing my mind," he said to the boy who was not there, shaking his head slowly as he went to see what Selma was up to.

ي‍

Tynor didn't know how he had gotten to the steps of the Summit library but he didn't give it any thought. He only knew he could do it, that's all. These sorts of "episodes" had been happening to him all his life; although lately they were getting harder to control. Enough so his mom and some of his teachers had noticed, thus, the visits to Dr. Warren. Of course everyone thought he was lying when he said he didn't know. They assumed he was taking drugs or that he was depressed and needed drugs. Tynor did what he had always done. He rolled with the changes. If they wanted him to see a shrink, then he would see the shrink. "I'm pretty sure he's not listening," he told his mom. But then, she wasn't listening either.

He tossed the end of the carrot into a trash barrel next to the entry and pulled the heavy glass door open. A wall of cool still air washed over him, followed by the sweet smell of books, plastic, and new carpet. Still bopping to the music in his mind, he entered the main hall and wandered over to the periodical rack.

The new Rolling Stone was in. Keith Richards, looking more than ever like a grisly ancient pirate, grinned back from the cover. "All right then," he whispered as he pulled the glossy magazine out of the wooden stick it hung from. Nearby, there was an empty over-stuffed leather chair with his name on it.

Tynor read the first few columns of an article about corruption in Congress. He was distracted by an advertisement for some sort of Budweiser Beer cruise with a photo of a beach in Jamaica. "That's what I'm talking about," he said out loud to himself. The librarian at the reference desk shot him an ugly glance. "I'm so down with that!" Tynor tapped the page with his pointer finger.

The librarian, a frumpy matron in muu-muu-like sack dress put her finger to her lips just like a cartoon parody of a librarian and hissed a loud "Shsssh."

Tynor ignored her. He flipped through a few more pages, skimming the articles, looking for the feature about the Stones. He didn't notice the black-haired girl until she was kneeling right there beside him.

"Jagger is an old fart," she said quietly, reading over his shoulder. "He's as old as my dad, and *he's* an old fart," she continued.

Tynor pulled his dark glasses off his face and, untangling them from his hair, stuffed them into the inside pocket of his leather jacket. He looked at the side of the girl's white face framed by her shoulder-length black hair. She wore a black tank top and black jeans. He noticed that the shirt was tight, but her breasts were little and it didn't seem to matter. There was a jeweled stud in the side of her left nostril.

"Yeah, but he's *Mick-fucking-Jagger*, right?" Tynor replied.

"Young man. *This*," Muu Muu waved both hands in front of her as though she were raising the mists, "is a library. *Not* a social club." She glared. Tynor noticed she wore horn rimmed glasses. His grandmother wore the same type.

Both Tynor and the girl erupted, hands over mouths, unable to suppress their giggles.

"Out," the librarian shouted, pointing toward the door. Other readers looked up at her to see what the disturbance was. Tynor stuffed the magazine inside his coat and looked at his companion.

"Let's split, right?"

As they left, the laughter they could not contain spilled out and echoed in the main hall. They skipped down the steps and crossed

Main Street to the city park next to the Erie Lackawanna commuter train station.

Tynor said, "My dad used to take that train into the city every day. When I was little I used to wish he would take me with him in the morning. One day I wished so hard that I could ride that big green train that I just fainted."

"Really? You actually fainted?"

"I guess, 'cause when I woke up I was on the train, sitting next to my dad. I was so glad he'd come back and taken me with him I reached over and hugged him."

"Aw, that's cute."

"No, not really. He was pissed. He got off at the next stop and took the train back home. He didn't talk to me or nothing, just grabbed me by the wrist and dragged me off the train. When we got home he and my mom were yelling and shit. They split up pretty soon after that. I always liked that train though." He looked over at her. She was eyeing him.

"You are a strange boy. What's your name, Rolling Stone?"

"Wouldn't that be cool? Nah, my name's Tynor, the first part for my grandpa, he was named Tyler, Tyler Hewett. The second part is for my other grandpa Norton, Norton Smyth."

"Are you a Hewett or a Smyth?"

"Actually, I'm a Mann. My mom had two fathers, and my dad wanted to call me Thomas after himself. My mother didn't want anything to do with it. At least that's what she tells me. What's your name?"

"You can call me Red. It's not my real name, but that's what everybody calls me."

Tynor looked at her sideways, glancing at her black hair.

She continued, "It's a long story. Don't ask."

"Well, I'm glad to make your acquaintance, Red."

23

"Charmed I'm sure, Mr. Mann."

"Just call me Tynor, ok? That Mr. Mann shit is going a little too far."

"Touchy, aren't we?" she said, cocking her right eyebrow.

"Hey, how'd you do that?"

"What?"

"Make your eyebrow go up like that."

"Like this?" She cocked the right, then the left, then the right again. They dissolved into giggles.

Tynor pulled the stolen magazine from his coat and opened it on his lap. He and Red sat quietly reading together. He would look over at her when he was ready to turn the page. She would nod or shake her head without taking her eyes off the type. They read like that for a few minutes. A train pulled into the station, its whistle shrill and wheels screeking to a stop. The conductor yelled something in conductor speak that neither of them could understand.

The ad with the Jamaican beach was on the next page. Tynor said, "I would like to go there someday. I just love that beach."

Red murmured something, nodding. Tynor couldn't make out the words. He stared up at the blue sky and the white sand. In the photo a man and a woman were running near the surf holding hands. He felt a little dizzy; he knew what that signaled, so he began speaking to try and ward it off.

"Have you ever noticed that if you want to go somewhere you have to think about it first?"

Red looked at him with her eyes crossed.

"Well, duh!?"

"No, I mean it, hear me out. You have to imagine where you want to go before you can go there."

"Okay, I guess. What's your point?"

"Well, when you really want to leave, like if you are going to a great concert or, you know, like, going out to buy a dress you always wanted or something..."

"Hey, Mr. Mann, do I look like the kind of a girl that gets all wet over buying a new dress?"

Tynor blushed, and then recovered with, "Hey, stick to Tynor, 'k? My dad is Mr. Mann, and I am nothing like him. Besides, you know what I'm saying, right?"

"Yeah, I can get excited about going. Like if it's the night before we leave for vacation in Florida or something. When I was little I couldn't sleep at all the night before. I would dance around like I had to pee. I couldn't understand why we didn't just go already."

"That's what I mean," he went on, folding the magazine. Now only the beer advertisement showed. "When you really want to be somewhere, it kind of fills your mind. It makes sense because you have to imagine where you want to be if you want to go there, right?"

Red was just looking at him. Tynor was beginning to feel like he sounded crazy; he tried not to think about it and just plowed ahead. "Well, I believe when you start thinking that you are going some-where, there is a part of you that's already left."

"Like what part? Your soul?"

"I don't know exactly. Maybe we're not just one thing. Maybe we are a collection of parts. And maybe one part of us, our mind or soul or whatever you want to call it, is not stuck here the same way our bodies are. I have never felt comfortable in my body."

Red was nodding so Tynor went on. "Well, what if you just let your mind, or whatever it is, go on without you? Wouldn't your body just, sort of, follow it out there?"

"You are pretty crazy, Tynor Mann," she said, but she was smil-ing. She put her hand on his arm. He smiled looking up at the sky to try and find his place.

25

"Yeah," he said, glancing over at her. "So that's what I do."

He was silent. They continued smiling at each other.

"What?" Red said, still smiling.

"That's what I do. I just let my mind, or whatever, go where I want to end up and..."

"You're serious, aren't you?" She cocked her eyebrow again.

He continued, "... then my body follows me out there."

She looked at him, her smile fading. The train pulled out of the station. The whistle blew two short blasts and then one long.

Tynor's grin widened. "Here, I'll show you."

He held up the magazine so that they could both see the beach picture and no other part. He said, "Watch this."

It was sort of like the sounds of the traffic and the twittering of sparrows grew in volume. A mosquito buzzed in her ear, and Red removed her hand from Tynor's arm and swatted at it. He was staring at the picture. She looked at his half closed eyes. Somewhere at the edge of the park, a horn blared followed by a driver shouting obscenities. When Red looked back to the magazine it was lying on the grass. Tynor was gone.

She called his name. She felt the bench where he was sitting a moment before; it was still warm. She stood up and spun around. He was not walking away.

Vanished.

Her eye caught a glint of something on the lawn next to the bench. It was a pair of wrap-around dark glasses.

She turned them over in her hands as she walked toward home, out of the other side of the park, frowning. As she stepped onto the sidewalk Tynor walked right up alongside her from behind.

"Shit," she said, "You scared me, where the hell did you disappear to?"

"Jamaica. Didn't I tell you?"

26

"Oh right, I'm supposed to believe that." She was shaking; her voice was a little too loud, a little too high.

"Hey, I was looking for those." He plucked his shades out of her hand, twirled them around in his palm once before stuffing them back into his jacket. He reached his other hand into the outer flap pocket, and when he removed it, it was curled into a fist. "Well, here. I got you something. Hold out your hand."

Red did as she was told. In truth she didn't have the wits to resist. Her mouth was open, she closed it. She wanted to be angry.

Tynor turned his hand over and tipped it slightly. A thin stream of white sand poured into Red's open palm.

"Maybe you'd like to go somewhere with me," he said grinning.

Red raised her right eyebrow. "Yeah, maybe." She mumbled. "Yeah."

Sit, Roll Over, Speak

Carla held the tiny black terrier puppy up over her head. Its cute hind legs and tail dangled as he squirmed. He had a white blaze on his small chest that looked a little like a lightning bolt. The young dog fought for a moment and then relaxed and hung limp. In her imagination she pictured the dog's mother surrounded by several similar puppies nuzzling their way into her soft under-fur in search of full teats. She completed the picture by imagining her new puppy nuzzled in next to his brothers and sisters. Maybe I will call him Flash, for that funny white mark, she thought.

Carla put her new dog onto her lap. He was already asleep.

Flash became the center of the nine-year-old girl's life. He slept in his basket at the side of her bed (at least until her mom had closed the door after kissing her goodnight; then she scooped Flash and held him close to her chest under the covers). She made a ritual out of saying goodbye to him in the morning, and he was always waiting there to greet her when she arrived home from school. She knelt down to the little terrier and spoke to him sitting before her. The little dog looked right into Carla's eyes as though he was listening.

"I am going to be away all day, Flash." She pictured the sun moving quickly across the sky like in an animated crayon drawing. "After your breakfast," she imagined his little stainless steel bowl and the scrapey sound of peeling the metal lid from the can, "Mom will let you out into the backyard to do your business." She saw the blades of green grass from little Flash's point of view. "Then, you can play with your rubber squeaky ball."

"Soon it will be time for a nap. The mailman will push letters through the slot in the door." She remembered the mystery of letters and newspapers appearing through the metal flapper slot in the front door of the house when she was a smaller girl. "But don't you bark, you hear? You'll be a good dog, and before the sun goes down," the same image of the yellow crayon sun moving across the arc of the blue crayon sky, "I will be home."

She scratched him behind both ears and stood up, turned and left without another thought.

Flash did not whine or complain. He acted as though he understood every word.

Flash was small and well-behaved enough to travel with Carla pretty much wherever she went. When he was still a tiny puppy she would even bring him into the grocery store in her coat pocket when she went shopping with her mom. After he was a year old, she would make him stay in the car. Carla would warn him when she was going to be leaving him.

"Carla. Why do you insist on speaking to Flash as though he's a person?" her mom asked on the way to the dry cleaners.

"But he understands me."

"I think you are too old to be speaking to a dog all the time."

Carla thought about it while they sat waiting for the signal light to turn green. An old woman with a walker crept across the four lanes of stopped traffic, a look of intense determination on her wrinkled face. A horn honked from somewhere. Carla looked down at the small dog sitting attentively in her lap and thought, Maybe I should just send you pictures, Flash.

❧

From that point on, Carla was careful not to speak out loud to Flash. She continued to send him pictures. At the end of dinner one evening, as Carla was finishing up the last of her meatloaf, Flash excitedly stood up on his hind legs and hopped at her mom's chair.

Carla's mom said, "Just for that, I'm not going to give any to you."

"What?" Carla asked.

"Well," her mom replied, beginning to clear the table, "I was thinking about giving Flash my scraps, and he got excited." She stopped and looked down at the little terrier still sitting on the floor next to her chair. He gave a tentative wag. "You stay out of my head, little dog. If I want to say something to you, I will say it out loud."

Carla realized that her mom wouldn't admit that Flash could read her thoughts. Grownups are confusing, she thought. I'm not supposed to talk to my dog, but it's okay if she does. Carla put her plate in the sink. "I'll give you a treat later," she said to Flash silently. "You better go lay down out of sight."

❧

Flash was always afraid of thunder and needed special reassurance from Carla during storms. Even after he was a teen-aged dog of four ("about sixteen in dog years," Carla would explain), Flash would tremble and whine when lightning lit up the night sky. Inevitably several seconds later the thunder would roll, low and growling or sharp and explosive. The little dog was inconsolable during these episodes, pushing his trembling, cold nose beneath Carla's hip under the covers as though she could protect him from the sound by sitting on him.

Carla tried different images, but nothing seemed to help. During one such storm, she was sending him pictures of sunny fields of tall grass. The tips of the stalks were bending as a wave of light air blew across them. The thunder was close and particularly loud. The windows of her room rattled. Carla, normally a calm child, was shocked by its ferocity.

When she gripped the little dog and pulled him to her chest, she heard a young man's voice clearly in her thoughts say, *You don't have to be afraid, I love you.*

Carla instantly forgot her shock and switched on the light.

Holding Flash under his front legs, she looked directly into his warm brown eyes and said, "Was that you, Flash? Did you speak to me?" The little terrier wagged his tail and licked at her nose.

The South Hills shopping mall was packed shoulder-to-shoulder with after-Christmas shoppers. The guy in the big, grey, wool coat was really just a teenager. He wore a knit winter stretch cap pulled over his ears so you could not see his shaved head. His thick dark eyebrows and height made him look older than he was. Sweat beaded on his pale forehead, but he shivered, wiping at his runny nose with the coat's dirty sleeve. His parents had named him Mitchell, but nobody in his shrinking circle of friends knew him by that name anymore. His "brothers," as he thought of them, called him Mick.

Carla was there with her friends Melissa and Gabby sitting at the food court and drinking Cokes, as was their Saturday ritual. A little later they were going to return some Christmas presents. Gabby's grandma always gave her bulky reindeer sweaters from Sears. They were planning on taking the refund money over to American Eagle or Journeys to see what kind of cool gifts they could trade for. As usual, Carla kept Flash in his suitcase-like dog carrier. Mall security knew Flash from years of such weekend outings, and as long as he was not running loose they weren't concerned with him. He was normally so silent that few people even knew he was there.

The girls did not see the tall man-boy in the wool coat as he shuffled by them at the Chick-Fil-A. As he passed by, Flash began a low growl in the back of his throat.

Carla shook his carrier and said, "Shush." She and the girls had been talking about that boy, Tynor Mann, who was a couple of grades older. He wandered the halls in a black beret and sunglasses, nodding his head to an unheard beat. Gabby thought he was crazy. Carla insisted that he was "crazy cool." There was no space for the little dog in this conversation. Flash continued to growl more quietly. Carla ignored him.

Mick knew his brothers were watching. He did not know where they were, but they were always close during an initiation. It was hard to walk. The drugs were bubbling through his arteries now, teasing at the edges of his brain, making him want to laugh and cry at the same time. His nose ran nonstop, unheeded. His target was the fat bastard who ran EarthBound Trading, a store that sold cheap imported silk and Indian print cloth, carved wooden elephants and junk along with glass pipes and papers. The bastard shortchanged Mick's brother, Stack, in a deal involving a half pound. Cheating one brother was the same as cheating every brother.

Mick was sent to set the scales to right. He and Stack had filed the serial number off a stolen Mossman pump-action twelve gauge and hacksawed the barrel down to five inches. The Mossman came with interchangeable pistol and shoulder stocks, making it a perfect candidate for a deadly concealed weapon. Mick had it loaded with seven shells and stuck down inside his high engineer's boot on the right side. The short barrel made it useless for hunting birds, but for close range it would spray a wide and indiscriminate sweep of lead shot in the direction it was fired. The gun looked like something Mad Max would use—held in one hand and shot like a revolver. It was pre-pumped and ready to fire the first blast. Mick associated the sound of pumping the gun with feelings of God-like power. That sound (and the black and yellow capsules he and Stack ate like jelly-beans) made him feel invincible.

Flash began scratching the bottom of his carrier as though he were attempting to dig a hole.

"What is your problem, little man?" Carla puzzled just as he snapped the door latch open and hopped out of the box, scrambling onto the smooth floor. The dog began barking in his high-pitched terrier voice.

Carla launched out of her chair, spilling her twenty-ounce Coke onto the floor and causing the other kids seated nearby to jump away from the splashing liquid. Her feet slipped as she ran around the corner and into the crowd, yelling after the dog that was now twenty feet ahead of her and disappearing into the forest of shoppers' legs.

She closed the gap between them quickly, deftly weaving between the bulky-coated masses, and dove the last five feet, scooping up the agitated dog directly in front of the EarthBound store. Flash struggled to get free, squirming against Carla's body. She was out of breath and could not clear her mind to send a calming image. She was getting ready to chastise the dog when Flash suddenly stopped struggling.

Carla heard him clearly in her mind, "He has thunder; he is going to make thunder." Carla gasped. She saw the image of the gun shoved into his boot.

The tall man-boy in the wool coat turned. He was standing directly in front of her and the small black dog. They looked into each other's eyes. Mick sniffed loudly and Flash whined. Carla's mind filled with the image of the sawed-off Mossman pump action. Without thinking she yelled, "Oh my god, he's got a gun!"

Through the fog of his vision Mick detachedly realized that the girl was an obstacle to his goal. He imagined effortlessly sliding the shotgun from his boot and quickly dispatching both of them with one fluid motion. But the gun caught on the ragged edge of the top of his boot and, instead of sliding out smoothly, he pulled up on the trigger and his right foot exploded in a spray of mutilated leather, bones and blood.

Several people in the nearby crowd were wounded by stray shot, although most of the force from the blast was absorbed by the mall's cement floor or Mick's body in ricochet. He collapsed unconscious amid screams and panic in a widening pool of his blood.

A cloud of acrid smoke hung in the air, imitating a slow motion movie shot. The smoke drifted lazily around Carla's head. Though people were running in all directions away from the center of activity, Carla and Flash stood hardly moving in a freeze frame of inactivity. For a moment, time for them simply stood still.

They stared, unhurt, in wonderment at the boy sprawled before them, as the floor space around them cleared with the echo of the blast ringing in their ears.

Flash looked up at Carla, whose mouth and eyes were open wide. The little dog reached out and flicked her chin once with his tongue.

෴

A Day in the Life

Our art teacher's name was Mr. Whitehall, but he insisted we called him David. It was weird. David wore brightly colored shirts and bell bottom dungarees. That was what my mom called them. Later we called them Levis, and nowadays no one can remember calling them anything but blue jeans. It's funny the way the names change, but things stay the same. His hair was shaggy too, not as long as men's hairstyles became. Nevertheless it was long for a teacher in a small suburban New Jersey town in 1968. I've never thought about it before, but I wonder how he kept his job back then. He was like, the only teacher in middle school who could dress like that and get away with it. Maybe it was because he was the art teacher, and he was supposed to be *free* and *artistic*. Of course I spent the last two months of eighth grade in a coma on a respirator at Summit Metro Hospital, so for all I know they did fire him.

Eddie Hubbard and I sat together in Mr. Whitehall's, I mean, David's fourth period art class on Wednesdays. We were learning about woodcuts by making linoleum block prints. Eddie thought Albrect Durer, the eleventh century German artist, was the coolest illustrator who ever lived, and we spent most classes trying to draw the nurse, Mrs. Shaffer's, porky face, in place of one of the four horsemen of the apocalypse. I think she was pestilence. Durer is believed to have invented the cartoon. Eddie was one hell of a cartoon-ist.

David paid no attention to us. We were his star pupils. We spent *all* of our time drawing. Art class was like recess to us. Come to think of it, David didn't pay much attention to anyone in that class. After he explained our assignments for the six-week period, he would sit behind his desk most days sketching still lifes in stick charcoal on a monstrous pad of newsprint paper he kept clamped to a huge wooden easel.

It was David Whitehall who introduced us to Sgt. Pepper. I guess because it was the art classroom, which was way down at the end of the school building, he could also get away with playing music during class. This made him an instant hero to every kid in eighth grade. But listening to these songs during class only one day a week was not nearly enough for us. A couple of weeks into the woodcutting project, Eddie stole the record by throwing his jacket over it and stashing it behind a trashcan until the last bell rang.

We spent every available minute after school, and on weekends, locked in Eddie's tiny attic bedroom memorizing each of the songs. We even recorded the whole thing on cassette tapes so we could bring *Fixing a Hole* and *For the Benefit of Mr. Kite* into the woods with us when it got too hot to stay indoors. Summer was looming. The two of us were thirteen that year. We were just a little too old to play in tree houses and just a little too young to actually date the girls we spent all of our time talking about, at least when we weren't talking about what John Lennon and Paul McCartney really meant when they wrote about Lucy in the sky or getting high with the help of their friends.

I can't remember why I was standing on the railing of the second story platform of our tree house. The rickety contraption was nailed together from stolen lumber and junk salvaged from abandoned houses in a disused resort community a mile or so behind Eddie's house. Ladders were blocks of wood attached with a hundred ugly nails pounded into the five birch trees that made up the foundational posts. The roots pushed up large rocks and intertwined with each other, knotting the ground around the building site. We attached railings waist-high around the flat roof. I was probably balanced twenty-eight feet above the rocky soil.

Few branches grow low on birch trees. The forest canopy towered above our meager fortress. Any limbs that remained were useless to build on, having been deprived of sunlight for decades; they might look like branches, but they were more like dead sticks that had not fallen off yet.

Eddie and I bantered and sang bits of *It's Getting Better*.

"I don't know if it's getting better or not," Eddy said. "My dad came home drunk last night, and he and my mom had a screaming match until dawn. I woulda came out here if the crickets didn't make so damn much noise." He guzzled NeHi orange soda from a glass bottle.

We snuck out to sleep in our fort once the last summer, but the sound of a billion insects was too loud for us suburban boys. I was lucky when I came back home; my dad had gotten up to pee, and I almost got caught sneaking back in.

The next song on our homemade cassette tape was *A Day in the Life*. John Lennon's nasal tenor echoed across the empty woods as we climbed up on the flat roof. We lay on our backs peering up through the late spring greenness. Saturday afternoon clouds drifted above us like cotton balls on the surface of a creek. I guess I was bored, I climbed up on the railing. The middle, bridge section of the song approached. The tape had gotten tangled once, and the slight garbling made the mid-song orchestral crescendo even more otherworldly and disorienting.

I asked Eddie, "When he says that part about finding his way upstairs and having a smoke, do you think he's talking about pot?"

"Nope," Eddie said, pulling a rumpled Marlboro out of his shirt packet. "He's talking about a ciggy." He made his voice all high and squeaky when he said *ciggy* and continued in an extreme British accent, "D'you want a toke, bloke?"

He struck a paper match with one hand using his thumb to bend it over and ignite it without pulling it out of the book, and touched fire to the tip of the sorry looking butt. Then he grinned with the cigarette clenched between his teeth and squinted at me, shaking his head quickly from side to side. I began to chuckle.

Eddie was always a clown. With that maniacal joker's grin pasted to his face, he began duck-stepping across the tree house roof. By the time he reached the tree and spun around like a wind-up tin soldier, I was laughing so hard I couldn't catch my breath. I began to jump down off of the railing and extended my center of gravity a little too far behind. Instinctively I reached up and grabbed that one branch for balance. I remember looking at it clenched in my fist as I fell backward to the packed-hard earth.

I blinked. Sunlight slanted through venetian blinds, casting orange stripes on the beige carpet. I had a newspaper in my lap. I sighed and wondered, what was I just thinking about? The Sgt. Pepper album was playing somewhere nearby. John Lennon crooned about reading the news. I looked down at the paper. There was a picture of a totally smashed police cruiser with an inset picture of a beefy man, grinning red-faced, wearing a policeman's cap. A crowd of gawking bystanders surrounded the wreck.

I began to read the cover story about a local cop, Randy Dugger, who had been voted fastest swimmer in the summer games. The article described the traffic accident that claimed his life.

I looked at his picture again. Beefy face; sad eyes. The caption read: Celebrated officer runs red light.

The doorbell rang. I dropped the paper on the floor and opened the front door, but no one was there.

"Hello?" I called into the growing darkness and thought, when did it get dark? A little shiver itched between my shoulder blades. I looked around outside on the small porch.

The song was still playing, maybe from the radio in a passing car, or somewhere inside the house...

Our house sits on a little hill and the neighborhood stretches out in front. Across the street a mist began to rise as the heat of the day faded, replaced by the cool damp air of evening. It was an eerie scene: Lonely houses, shrouded in dusk, fog obscuring any details close to the earth. The Baxter's old 35-millimeter projector was set up and a movie was showing on the exterior wall of their garage. They had done this in the summer as entertainment for all the kids on the block for as long as I could remember. I walked toward their house. Ghostly black and white images danced on the siding.

Their side yard was set up with rows of lawn chairs; they were all empty. The projector sat on top of their picnic table, clicking and flashing. The iconic clock tower of Big Ben chimed as images of several thousand people ran through the streets of London. Soldiers threw their World War Two English army helmets into the air. I recognized the story, but I couldn't place any of the actors.

I sat in one of the chairs and watched. For some reason the only soundtrack was the same Beatles song, singing about being turned on...

The movie just went on and on. My eyelids drooped. My thoughts were cold honey, slow and sluggish: Where was everyone? Why was Mr. Baxter showing foreign films in the spring on a school night? Why was the only soundtrack a song from the Beatles Sgt. Pepper album? I drifted off.

≈

I woke up on the floor of my bedroom with a sharp pain in my shoulder, and that song—that damn Beatle's song was still playing. I stumbled to the bathroom with the nagging feeling that I was supposed to be somewhere. I looked at my face, puffy in the mirror. The smell of coffee drifted upstairs. I never drink the stuff, but it smelled so good I decided to try some. The hot, black liquid was bitter and disgusting. I wondered aloud, "Why do people drink this stuff?"

My mother's cuckoo clock startled me and I had that feeling again: Where am I supposed to be? I wandered outside looking for my bike.

Mrs. Collier's big boat of a Chrysler Newport pulled up to the curb at the end of my driveway. The horn honked. The window was rolled down and I could see her waving at me to come over to the car. As I walked to the end of the driveway I glanced up and down the street. Something wasn't right.

It was early and neighbors were dragging garbage cans or watering gardens. The morning sun cast long, sharp-edged shadows across the dark green lawns. Mr. Stanley, wearing a torn bathrobe and a dazed look, shuffled up the walk, paper in hand.

When I reached the street the Chrysler was gone, replaced by a huge idling school bus. The driver called out to me, "Hey kid hurry up. We ain't got all day y'know."

The other seats on the bus were occupied by men dressed in identical suits and ties. I wondered, why are all these businessmen riding on a school bus? We turned the corner onto Phillips Street, and then we were downtown stopped in front of a tall glass and aluminum office building.

I followed the crowd of suited men inside and up a broad marble staircase to a mezzanine overlooking the foyer.

The same song, *A Day in the Life,* was playing in the lobby. I bumped into the guy in front of me, but he didn't seem to notice. I said, "Sorry," but it didn't feel as though anyone could hear me. I was really getting nervous. Wait, this was familiar. I knew something had happened, but I couldn't remember what it was.

At the top of the landing a woman in a navy blue suit gave me a cigarette from a red pack and then lit it with a silver lighter. I heard a man say, "Eldorado." I inhaled deeply, even though I don't smoke. For some reason I recalled the image of my friend, Eddy.

I stood there gazing around the people moving about on the landing. I could tell that something wasn't right, but I couldn't quite get the thought to form. It was as though I had an itch on my back and no matter how hard I tried, I just couldn't reach. My mind drifted through the strange events of the morning. I couldn't remember getting dressed. Maybe, I thought, this is just some weird dream.

The song continued playing. The singer was reading the news again. As people milled around on the short pile carpet, I made my way to a leather lounge chair and picked up the newspaper folded on its arm. I sank into the deep cushions and read: 4000 holes in Blackburn, Lancashire.

Whoa, déjà-vu, I thought. I could hear each word in my mind before I read it. Then I was startled by a tap on my shoulder from a man in blue jeans and a green, cable-knit wool sweater.

The music abruptly stopped.

He had a shaggy haircut and a thick mustache. Bright brown eyes sparkled at me through a pair of round, metal-framed glasses. With a crooked grin and a thick British accent, he said, "Do you mind if I have me paper back, son?"

I held the paper up to him, and he folded it under his arm. As he began to turn I recognized him.

"Hey, you're John Lennon," I said, getting to my feet.

I pumped his hand up and down, staring up into his face. I rambled on, "Wow, I am *so* glad to meet you. What are you doing here?" Part of my mind wondered where *here* was, since I couldn't actually remember how I'd gotten there. But I kept talking the whole time, and Lennon was letting me shake his hand, just smiling at me like I was making sense. "I'm a really big fan," I continued. "I love Sgt. Pepper's. Every song is amazing, just amazing. I just can't believe this. I'm really talking to John Lennon."

My hand continued to pump. I stood there beaming; he just smiled down at me. After a moment he said, "So, can I have me hand back?"

"Oh, sure," I said, letting go and stepping back, having realized that my palm was sweating.

He wiped his hand on his pant leg and looked over his shoulder toward the stairway.

"Are you waiting for someone?" I had visions of Ringo, Paul, or George coming up the stairs. A bevy of Japanese girls dressed in plaid skirts carrying metal lunch boxes crested the top step.

"Me? Oh no, mate. I was just wondering..." He paused and looked over his shoulder again, the grin fading slightly. "Can you tell me where we *are*?"

For a moment I saw something in his face; it was like a raven's shadow crossed his features. He was still smiling, but the expression now seemed pasted on.

I was suddenly cold. I tried to think about how I had gotten here, but it was like bumping into a wall in the dark. I could recall drinking coffee and riding the bus. It was all wrong somehow. And then there was that song. Up until a moment ago it was playing all the time. Panic filled my chest. The air on the landing felt damp and misty. All the hard edges began to bleed like a fog was filling the room.

I tried to speak; I wanted to tell John that we were in Morris Township, New Jersey, but I knew that was a lie. I tried to tell him my name. All I could do was moan. A deep drumming grew louder. Though I did not hear it begin, I felt it in my feet. The throbbing in my head matched its rhythm. The pain grew heavier as the details of the room and people blurred and faded.

I tried one last time to speak: "John? Can you hear me? My name is Caleb Ross." But I couldn't tell if I'd made any sound. My ears were filled with other noises: Metallic clanking sounds, a rhythmic beeping, a sucking and swooshing, and hushed voices.

Then I heard my mother sounding a little too high-pitched and out of breath. She said, "Caleb, can you hear me? Caleb." I tried to open my eyes; they felt weighted with lead sinkers. There was something in my mouth, I tried to speak again; all that came out was mumbling and groans. I couldn't swallow. I began to panic, but everything felt wrapped in wool. I was numb.

My mom said, "Caleb, don't try to speak, you are on a respirator. Honey, can you open your eyes?"

I strained, but I was exhausted. I rested. Confused questions flooded my thoughts. How did I get here? I tried hard to remember, but it only made my head hurt. The clicking and swooshing sound cycled. My chest filled with air and deflated. I tried again to open my eyes, and I found myself in the upstairs lobby again, standing in front of John Lennon. He smiled warmly and said, "It's really okay Caleb, I'll wait here for you mate." He winked and messed up my hair.

I smiled and thought, This is real. John Lennon remembers my name!

But I was so tired. I couldn't even open my mouth to say thanks. My eyes drooped shut and when I tried to open them again they were stuck. I tried again and got a crack of blurred light, and then a little more. The room was out of focus. I was more exhausted than I have ever been in my life. My mom was sitting next to the hospital bed. I was surrounded by towers of equipment, tubes, flashing lights and steel poles. She said, "You rest now honey, you've had a big day."

I realized that our tape of *A Day in the Life* was playing on my cassette player somewhere in the room; I heard that patch of garbled tape.

I wanted to tell Mom that this was the best day of my life and that I'd met John Lennon, but I knew I couldn't speak. I let my mind drift, feeling as though I was falling backward down a sink drain, spinning away into the dark.

In the distance I heard the last strains of the song, *"I'd love to turnnnn, yoooo, onnnn..."*

The light in the room contracted quickly to a pinpoint and then,

Just...

Blinked...

Out.

❧☙

Hey, This is it, I'm Going to Die

I heard a story once that explains how I know. There was this missionary visiting some African tribe who observed a native mother. Children out there were carried around by their moms all the time. Every so often, with no verbal clues, this tribeswoman holds her diaperless little boy out at arm's length over a bush. The little wiener relieves himself, just like that.

After a day of following them around, the missionary can't keep her mouth shut. She asks, "How do you know when your baby has to pee?" The native mom looks at her, surprised for a second, and then bursts out laughing; perfect teeth flashing, her eyes squeezed shut. She doubles over and can't breathe. Finally she wipes her eyes and says, "How do *you* know when you have to pee?"

That's kind of how it is here. I just know. I'm dead, and that's that.

Now, how I got here? That's a horse of different color.

I drive, or, *drove* a cab in Manhattan. I was rushing this fare to Idlewild—that's Kennedy International to all you kids—up the B-Q-E when traffic, for no apparent reason, comes to a complete standstill. This happens with nauseating regularity on most of the chuck-hole-riddled, major arteries in the Rotten Apple. We're sitting there with our thumbs up our butts. Horns are blaring, temperature gauges start creeping up. After a moment I spot the cause of our detainment: About a hundred feet up on the opposite side of the guardrail there's a three-car pile-up.

No one seemed to be hurt, yet. The drivers of all three cars were standing in the middle of the West bound lane screaming at each other. Face to face. One guy looked like he was a boil about ready to pop. His face so constricted by his once-white collar that the veins and arteries are backing up blood into his sweaty, sausage-like face. The smaller guy had on an absurd checkered jacket. The sleeves were way too short, and his bare forearms were sticking out of the cuffs, waving in the air like antennae. There was a cigarette butt pinched up in the crook between the index and middle fingers of his right hand.

The third driver was a short, old, white-haired woman. She was screaming so loud I could hear her shrill obscenities even with my windows closed, above the horns. A gray poodle was squished up under her right arm and she was poking the black-leather gloved index finger of her left hand in the boil-man's face. She was so out of control spittle hung from her bony chin; I heard something about how they were all cocksucker sons of whores. The dog barked non-stop. Every so often she gave it a squeeze like some clogged up, mangy bagpipe and yelled "shut-the-fuck-up, Trixie." This caused the poodle to gag and wheeze for a beat before it started up again.

Usually I wait it out and watch the show—it's not my dime, ya know? But that day my fare was itchy, and he had cash. He shoved a crisp fin under the Plexiglas wall separating us and told me to go around. I grabbed the bill and saw my chance. I knew I could get around the rubberneckers; we were only a few cars back. I gassed it into the shoulder and plowed through some garbage. My right wheels ran up on the cement curb. I only just kissed the iron fence and the concrete wall off the shoulder, went up four or five cars, and back onto clear road. I wouldn't even have to make out a report on that little scratch.

It's a strange thing to see an eighteen-wheeler fly. This one crashed through the guard rail of the overpass ahead of us. It seemed to fall out of the sky. All the sound and heat and dirt around me seemed to suck away somewhere. Silence. All I could see was the graceful arc in midair of the cab and trailer, all of its wheels still turning. I could read the side of the trailer: GOD - Guaranteed Overnight Delivery, lettered in fire-engine red. I opened my mouth to speak to my fare. I was going to say, "Hey, would you look at that." Then everything slid into slow motion. The mouths of the three drivers gaped open, their necks twisted, heads following the spectacle of a flying semi. Even the yapping dog watched.

I thought, Hey, this is it. I'm going to die.

The plummeting big rig veered toward us and fell right into my lap. My windshield imploded and the grillwork of the Peterbilt rushed in to greet me. When that truck hit the hood of my cab the silence broke. Time resumed normal speed. Glass sprayed like a garden hose. My fare screamed like he was being burned alive. Maybe he was.

All I could do was watch. I felt nothing. I was awake with my eyes open, like watching a movie. The carnage unfolded around me with each event separate and clear, although occurring simultaneously. I saw colors and lights. I smelled diesel fuel and hot macadam. I even smelled the vinyl of my cab seats. I heard the metal tear like a tortured tin shack being blown apart around my head. The radio played American Pie.

The last thing I saw was this little girl standing on the patio of a building adjacent to the roadway eating an ice cream cone. It looked too big for her. She was wearing a white summer jumper with big blue and green flowers on it. Her hair was braided in two blond pig-tails. I was concerned the chocolate would stain her dress.

Badger Will Lead You Home

"You stay right here, Tommy Stewart. Don't you move."

His mom was changing his little sister, Sara. She's always changing that baby, he thought. The park bathroom was stinky. Tommy scrunched up his nose and said, "P-U." He crouched down to look under the stall. He could see white-socked ankles poking out of sneakers; a pair of panties printed with red daisies lay crumpled on top of the shoes. The lady in the stall farted loudly. Tommy giggled and looked up at his mom. He grasped her pant leg with his pudgy fingers.

"Dat lady faahted," he whispered.

Marlene Stewart was busy. She did not respond to her toddler.

She had discovered what she and the children affectionately called a "monster poop" in little Sara's diaper. The baby was already strapped into the Koala.

"Oh, crap," she muttered, realizing that she was out of baby wipes. The paper towel dispenser and the sinks were ten feet away. A twist of her hair escaped the braid at the back of her neck and dangled in her face. She blew it out of the way, but it drifted back into her eyes. Little Sara, who didn't like to be on her back under the best of circumstances, began to cry. Marlene tried to push the hair out of her face again with the back of her wrist, but it was too late.

49

The wisp tickled her nose, setting off a chain reaction of sneezes. She unconsciously put her hand up to cover her mouth and smeared a bright orange stripe of monster poop across her cheek.

Frustrated and disgusted, she cinched the changing table belt tight around her now screaming daughter's middle and crossed the filthy restroom floor to wash her hands and grab a brown paper towel. It would only take a second.

By the time she turned back to the changing table, Tommy was gone.

Tommy Stewart, two and half feet tall, did not like the smelly bathroom. He was angry because his mom was changing Sara and ignoring him *again*. There was no door on the park's restrooms, just a cinder block partition wall. He wandered around the corner and into the bright, hot sunlight. His shadow appeared on the cement sidewalk in front of him. It slid across the dirt edging and into the bright green grass as he walked. He became captivated by the contrast of his shadow's deep dark green and the adjacent sunny grass. The heat of that sun beat on the back of his neck.

There were children laughing. He could see them on the swings across the playing field. He began to run toward the sound, shadow already forgotten. The laces had come untied on his red sneakers, and before he had gone more than a few yards he tripped, falling into the fragrant lawn. A grasshopper jumped off the blade directly in front of his nose. Laughing out loud, he scrambled to his feet and chased after the bouncing insect. Within two or three bounces the grasshopper disappeared into the woods bordering the park lawn. Tommy toddled into the cool dark woods. The grasshopper perched on a low branch. Tommy, imitating a cartoon he had once seen of a kitten stalking a butterfly, crept up to the green bug until his nose was almost touching it. It sprang away. Tommy's feet shuffled through the deep leaf bed. He picked up a stick and waved it like a sword. A crow broadcast an insult at him. He dropped the stick, startled and looked up to see where it was. He saw the rows of trees. He didn't hear any children. A blue jay launched like crumpled paper from a nearby birch. The only other sounds were bird songs in the distance and the gurbling of a nearby stream.

"Mommy?" Tommy said, turning around slowly. He sniffed.

He was surrounded by trees as far has he could see. Fear flooded his chest like cold water. The feeling scared him more than being alone. He began to cry.

After a few moments, it was too difficult to stand, and he dropped down hard in the dry leaves. Tommy's crying turned into a wail, his eyes squeezed tight. After a few breaths he fell over on his side as his crying subsided. He fell into a deep sleep punctuated by a few shuddering hitches.

When Tommy opened his eyes he was in shadow and the air had cooled. Goose bumps rose on the groggy child's bare arms. His face was pressed into the thick bed of the forest floor which filled his nose with fresh earth and the sweet tang of decaying oak leaves. A grey squirrel sat directly in front of him. Its little hands gripped one another. It tipped its head to the side, showing Tommy one black eye bead.

Tommy said, "Hi, Mr. Squirrel."

The squirrel said, "Hello, little boy. What are you doing here?"

Tommy sat up. He had seen many talking squirrels on TV. This was familiar to him, a little weird, but not too scary. He shivered and brushed the leaves from his shoulder. A breeze blew over the forest and the light darkened a note. He said, "I think I got lost." Tommy felt like crying again, but the squirrel's presence kept his fear down. He said, "Mr. Squirrel, do you know where my mommy is?"

The squirrel used his right hand to rapidly scratch behind his ear. The motion of the furry little paw was a blur. Tommy laughed.

The squirrel said, "I don't know your mommy. But I can help you find someone who might. Can you walk?"

"Sure," Tommy said, scrambling to his feet. "But I have short legs, so I can't go fast."

The squirrel hopped off without a reply, twitching his tail as if to say, "Come on, little boy, let's go this way!" He would hop a few feet and wait, looking back over his shoulder. They went on this way for several minutes. The sky grew darker. Tommy was a little afraid, so he began telling himself a story. He thought, this old squirrel lives in the forest. He must know where he's going.

But Tommy's little legs began to get tired and it was getting hard to see. He called out to the furry animal hopping a few feet ahead of him, "Hey, Mr. Squirrel, I'm afraid of the dark. I'm tired."

The squirrel turned back to him, and though Tommy could hardly make out his silhouette in the fading dark, he saw the tiny paw beckoning and heard, "The moon will be out soon and it's not much farther. Keep close. I will wait for you."

And the moon rose big and orange through the trees and the forest was illuminated. Each leaf seemed to be lit with its own silver spot light. It was easier to see than during the day. The squirrel kept his word and waited for the boy to catch up every one or two hops.

The twitchy grey animal stopped at a huge hollow oak tree and used his fist to knock on the wood next to the opening. From inside Tommy could hear an old grouchy voice; it reminded him of his grandpa.

The old voice said, "Who is it knocking on my door at this hour on a full moon?"

"Tis I, Grey Squirrel," said the squirrel.

A big spikey-haired head poked out of the hole in the hollow tree and startled Tommy. He stepped back and fell on his butt.

Squirrel continued, "And I brought a friend. This is a little boy with red feet." Squirrel bowed a deep bow. He turned to Tommy and, putting his hand to the side of his mouth, he said, "This is Papa Badger. He is very old and a smidge deaf. He will know how to find your mommy."

Papa Badger said, "Hurrumph. A boy. No good ever came from a *boy*."

"But he is lost," Squirrel replied, raising one eyebrow. "You know the code."

"Hmmm. The code, eh? Yea, I know the code." He waddled out into the moonlight. His coat was black with broad bands of grey that shinned in the moonlight. His eyes were milky with cataracts and his whiskers were wilted and bent toward the ground, unlike the squirrel whose whiskers stuck straight out like a starburst. Tommy thought Papa Badger looked tired. "I am bound to help you, little boy with red feet." He nodded his shaggy head and moved off into the underbrush. "Better keep up."

Tommy said, "But Mr. Squirrel, aren't you coming?"

"No. You go with Papa Badger now. He can show you." He scratched behind his ear again. "If anyone can." Squirrel scampered away, calling back, "See you again little boy with red feet. Good luck!"

It was not hard to keep up with Papa Badger. He moved so slow-ly that Tommy kept bumping into his wide flat butt and stubby tail. The boy was having fun; he talked almost non-stop to the badger. "I'm four years old. I am going to be five when the leaves begin to fall. Do you know how many that is?" He held up his right hand showing all the fingers. "I can count to five, too. One, two, three, four..."

Papa Badger was mostly deaf and could not hear Tommy. He said, "Just hold on to my tail so I know you're back there, boy." And Tommy did.

They reached a small stream of churning water and the badger began to cross, but Tommy let go of the tail and stopped. He knew better than to get his shoes wet. Mommy would be angry with him and yell. Papa Badger turned and said, "What's a matter with you boy? It's only a little water, won't hurt you none."

"My mom would be mad. I shouldn't get my shoes wet. I could catch 'moan-ya."

"Moan-ya? What's that?" the badger replied, very interested now. He had not eaten recently, and the prospect of catching a meal, even this unknown "moan-ya," made his mouth water.

"I don't know," Tommy said. "But I guess you get it from wet shoes or sumpthin. When mommy was talkin' about it I didn't think it was good."

"Alright, alright," Badger said as he waddled back across the little stream. You climb up on my back, and I'll carry you.

Tommy grabbed handfuls of badger fur and tried to pull himself up on to the broad back, but he was not strong enough. The badger lay down in a hollowed out dip in the leaf-strewn earth and bid the boy try again. Tommy half crawled, half climbed onto the wide back. Badger said, "Keep your hands knotted in my fur and I will carry you the rest of the way. It's not far now."

But the fun was wearing off. Tommy never stayed up at night and the badger's fur was warm and soft. Soon Tommy was sprawled out on his belly, asleep on Papa Badger's back.

❧

"Boy."

Tommy opened his eyes, but all he saw was fur.

"Boy," the badger was louder this time. "Time to go."

Tommy lifted his head and saw that they were at the edge of the woods now. There was a house across an expanse of lush lawn. Yellow light spilled from the windows onto the patio and walkway. Tommy blinked and slid down off the badger's back.

"Well, here you are. This is as far as I can go. 'Snot safe beyond the woods for badgers and such."

Tommy looked at the house. He said, "But this isn't my house. I don't know where I am."

"That's okay," Papa Badger said. "I have another friend who can take you the rest of the way."

A huge white furry dog padded silently around from behind them and sat panting in front of Tommy and the badger. Even sitting down the dog towered above the child.

"Boy with red feet, this is Marruke. She is a guardian dog. Marruke can walk between the world of the wild and the tame. She will lead you home."

"Do you talk, too?" Tommy asked Marruke .

"All beings talk, little man," she replied, and bowed her head to rub her soft fur against his face. "Grab a hold of my tail and I will take you."

Tommy said, "Goodbye, Papa Badger."

The badger had already waddled back toward the woods. He muttered "hurrumph" and disappeared into the darkness.

Marruke led Tommy to the front of the house and up the driveway to the sidewalk. The street was dark and the air began to chill.

Tommy whined, "Marruke, I'm cold. Can you keep me warm?"

"You can walk up close to my chest and put your arm over my back. That way the heat from my body will warm you."

For while they walked along the sidewalk in silence. The beams from the streetlights formed pools and Tommy dreamed with his eyes open that he and Marruke were wading through silver puddles. Tommy mumbled, "And I din' even get my feet wet." He was asleep on his feet.

The two walked up several side streets and alleys. Marruke could smell where the child belonged. She followed the invisible map through the back yards of the sleeping city.

Up ahead, on the corner, a uniformed police woman stood next to a white cruiser talking on her cell phone. When she saw the big white dog and the little boy stumbling alongside she stopped and stared for a moment. Then she said, "Hey Bill, I'll have to call you back. You are not going to believe what just came up the sidewalk."

Some Demons Don't Die

Mattie didn't think nothin' of it when John Cole shot the rooster. She heard the sharp report and stood out on the back porch, searching the barnyard for a moment. Once she caught sight of his 280 pounds rounding the corner of the barn, the neck of a limp, red-feathered bird clutched in one fist, his short barreled pistol in the other, she went back to scrubbing the kitchen floor, down on her knees with the wooden brush gripped in both hands.

She thought, He's been complainin' about too damn many roosters. I guess he finally got up off his fat ass and did sumpt'in 'bout it.

She pushed an errant strand of hair behind her ear with her index finger. Soapy water dribbled to the elbow. Pine Sol and old grease. John's heavy boots clomped up the back steps and across the worn threshold.

"Mind my scrubbin' the floor, John Cole. Don't you track no mud in here, you hear?"

The wooden screen door slammed. He dropped the bird onto the oak table. A red feather drifted through a dust mote in front of her face and settled on the drying floorboards.

"No good for nothin' but soup. Too old to roast," he said, going into the icebox. He pushed a few bowls and jugs around muttering, "Whars ma beer, Mattie?"

"You close that damn door, John Cole. All my food'll go bad with you refrigeratin' the whole house like that."

He snagged the remaining pop-top cans and marched out through the screen door. It slammed behind him; dry wood and rusty screen expelled a small cloud of dust into a beam. "Don't touch ma stuff, Mattie, I *tol'* you that before!" The smell of him lingered: Sour sweat, gear oil, and manure.

He clomped back down the steps. A few moments later, she heard his ancient International Harvester tractor wrench over and sputter to life, eventually receding as he drove out across the south pasture.

"Don't touch ma stuff," she mimicked, pursing her lips imitating his haughty stance. She sighed and absently touched a half-dollar-sized bruise below her left ear.

Mattie stared at the feather. Flies buzzed. The worthless bird would have to be dressed. She glanced at John Cole's muddy boot prints, sniffed, and stood up, dropping the brush, sloshing sudsy water over the pail. The feather swept beneath the refrigerator by the current.

The headless bird lay in a heap next to glass salt- and pepper-shakers. Blood puddled by a pile of mail from the past few days. Its clenched scaly yellow claws and iridescent red and green feathers glowed faintly in the fading sun. Flies crawled over the carcass and around the table, pausing to drink at the edge of the bloody pool like horses at a trough, their jerky movements a rhythm that Mattie could almost, but not quite, understand.

She forced her gaze away and moved to the sink. The pressure was low; it was a wonder there was water at all. Soon the well would dry up for summer. She blew the strand of hair out of her eyes and peered through the rotting window screen into the back yard: John Cole's back yard.

As the pot filled, she opened a box of wooden matches and lit a gas burner. The blue flame wavered for a moment and vanished. She struck another and held it to the small cloud of gas that collected around the burner. It ignited with a soft pop, singeing the fine hair on the back of her hand. The smell of sulfur, gas, and burned hair lingered in her nose.

She hefted the pot over to the stove and turned the gas to high, checking that the flame was still lit. Then she searched around in drawers and cabinets for her large knife, poultry shears, rubber gloves, a small glass bowl, a shopping bag, and a sheet of waxed paper.

The sun was below the horizon by the time the water was scalding. Mattie had filled another, smaller pot, and the water began to bubble. Gripping the rooster's legs in one gloved hand, she submerged the ruined bird in the boiling water and used a wooden paddle to hold its stiffening body under a few moments. She shook the excess water from the limp feathers and immediately set to pulling out large handfuls, stuffing them into the open paper bag.

She plucked like this until all but the smallest feathers were removed and the Rhode Island Red rooster was changed into a yellow skinned carcass. She burned the remaining pin feathers off by repeatedly passing it through the gas flame. Mattie thought about the transformation of a strutting, proud bully into dinner. Oh Mr. John Cole, I got yer dinner right here, she thought. A smile curled the corner of her small mouth.

Mattie made short work of the butchering. Heart, liver, lungs and gizzard were saved in the glass bowl; the remaining entrails and neck were piled on the sheet of waxed paper, a treat for the dogs. She quartered the bird, halved an onion, sliced two ribs of celery and a carrot and chopped the organs into a small dice.

She melted some lard in a cast iron pan and added the diced meat to it. When the soup regained its boil she lowered the gas, slid a dented lid over the pot, and stirred the sizzling meat with a metal spoon.

By the time orange sky faded to gray above the western horizon, Mattie had finished cleaning the kitchen. Chicken soup, and the scent of fresh dill she'd added as an afterthought, filled the air. She sat at the table in the almost dark, spooning the crispy organ bits onto saltine crackers and nibbling at them, her lips oily from the fat. The light of the passing sunset glowed faintly in the west windows, silhouetting her round face like a half moon.

John Cole ran the tractor and tended his few acres of sorghum. Aside from culling a rooster from time to time, the rest of the small farm was Mattie's providence. She was especially proud of her four Berkshire pigs: Three sows and a boar. After throwing the entrails to the dogs, she poured a bucket of slop into the pig's trough and marveled at how they reduced anything from onion peal to shank bones to dust in minutes. She watched them grunt and root. She shuddered.

The large knife would need sharpening. She took care of that first. Then, as was her custom, she meticulously gathered the rest of her supplies. The moon appeared bloated and bloodshot on the east horizon by the time she had everything collected in a large wicker basket. She wore a leather farrier's apron.

She moved the pigs, except one sow, into a smaller whelping enclosure just off the feeding pen and spread a large sheet of heavy plastic on the bare earth. John Cole's tractor rumbled in the distance across the field. She quickened her steps. Mattie pulled her daddy's 1873 Colt 45 Peacemaker from the basket and held the heavy gun up so the moonlight glinted off of its blued surface. The gravelly volume of the tractor increased. She figured he must be just around the side of the barn.

Mattie cocked the hammer back and gently rested the firearm in her deep apron pocket. She arranged a canvas oilcloth over the rest of the items in the basket. The still night air was scented by sweet magnolia mingled with rank pigs and oilcloth tang. She scratched the sow beneath her chin. The eight hundred pound beast, raised from a piglet by Mattie's hand, fell over on its side and grunted for more just as John Cole stomped around the corner.

"John Cole," Mattie cried. "Come yonder and see what's a matter with this here pig."

John Cole unlatched the wooden gate and lumbered over in the dim light. He said, "What?" and bent over, squinting at the moaning sow. Mattie stepped behind him and fired a single bullet into the back of his head near the base of his skull.

John Cole stood up and turned to her, the top section of his head gone from the fore to the crown. He burped once. She could smell the yeasty odor of beer mingled with decaying teeth. His eyes rolled up under his fleshy open lids and he flopped backward onto the sheet of plastic, twitching.

She used one of the boiled rooster legs to lure the sow back into the whelping pen and tossed the canvas away from the wicker basket. The Colt she wrapped in an old pillow case and removed her knife and several large black plastic bags.

"Oh, you are a bastard, John Cole, but you are dead bastard now."

She thought about spitting in his upturned face, but reconsidered, rubbing her neck with her left hand. He was a large animal, and she would be pressed to get him cut up before daybreak. Stretching the rubber gloves over the cracked, dry skin of her hands, she set to the task.

By the time the moon rose directly overhead, Mattie had cut off John Cole's clothes and stuffed them into one of the bags. The hardest part was pulling his teeth. She used a rusty old pair of pliers and put the broken molars and bicuspids in a pickle jar. She cut out the heart and put it in a small stainless steel bowl; the pigs would take the rest of him.

What meat she intended to keep was cut from the bones of his legs and haunches. She chuckled, thinking about rendering his fat into lard, but she never had any intention of keeping much of him. "Fixin' his bacon." She snorted.

By the time dawn stained the horizon, the fire in the burn can made from John Cole's clothes and the plastic sheet was almost out. Mattie filled the pickle jar with hydrochloric acid, kept around for cleaning the cement walkways after the mildew got them each summer, and the teeth dissolved after bubbling and steaming for a few minutes. She put it in the barn next to an old coffee can full of fat ticks and turpentine, mumbling, "Waste not, want not, John Cole"

The boar and sows were let back into the feeding pen and they made a short meal of what was left of him.

She lugged the bag of meat and the basket back into the house, unloaded and cleaned the gun, and stacked the meat into the chest freezer on the side porch. She put his heart onto the top shelf in the refrigerator, next to a jar of mayonnaise. Then she washed and put away her gloves and knife and used a wire brush to scrape down the leather farrier's apron.

Early sun already tinted the backyard. It made everything look like it was wrapped in orange cellophane—a clear sign that it was going to be another hot dry one. Mattie sat down at the old oak table and closed her eyes. "I jus' needs to rest a spell," she mumbled and immediately slipped into sleep, snoring within moments.

※

She woke up when the screen door slammed. The light switched on, blinding her momentarily. It took her a moment to realize where she was. The chicken soup simmered on the stove, the sweet scent of dill filled the room.

John Cole clomped off toward the bathroom saying, "Gotta pee, let's eat."

She stared at the knife gleaming in the drying rack and blinked at the bright incandescent glare. Mattie shook her head slightly, trying to clear away the haze of deep sleep.

Was it just a dream?

She shouted back, "All we got is this tough old rooster, though."

John Cole called from the other room, "Git me a beer, Mattie, I have me a powerful thirst."

Well hell be damned, she thought. If it was just a dry run then let's do it for real this time!

She ladled the steaming soup, and set the bowl out beside a glass. John Cole's boot steps approached. Grabbing the large kitchen knife from the rack, she opened the refrigerator with her back to him. His heavy clomping crossed the kitchen floor. The wooden chair creaked under his weight. With her head in the open refrigerator she whispered, "Give me strength..."

She found a beer can in the back and turned, kicking the refrigerator door closed with the side of her foot, the large knife clenched in her right hand.

John Cole, his bulky form bent over the soup, said, "You scrawny, good for nuthin, bitch. How you 'spect me to eat my dinner with no got-damn spoon?"

Mattie lunged at him screaming, "To the Devil with you, John Cole. I kilt you once, and I can kill you again!" She dropped the unopened can onto the wooden floor where it exploded, spraying and spinning, and with both fists gripping the handle, slammed the blade down into John Cole's hunched back.

Her hands and the knife passed through his body like he was smoke. The point collided with the bowl, shattering it and spraying soup. The force of her blow buried the tip deep in the oak table. Mattie realized that she could clearly see the spinning shards *through* him. Her breath caught in her throat. Testing, she waved her hand back and forth, scattering his image like a cold mist.

John Cole paid no mind. He stood slowly and turned to her. She now noticed that the top of his head was missing; the light from the fixture on the ceiling glowed through him like he was made of gauze. The strength in her legs drained and she collapsed to the floor, foamy beer puddled around her. Looking down at the wood planked floor on her hands and knees, her lank hair dangled in her face. She babbled, "Oh my God, sweet Jesus, what have I done?"

John Cole moved away from the table, the leg of his thick, mud-crusted overalls slicing through her side. It felt like ice-cold worms crawling through her belly. As the sound of his heavy boots clomped away, he said, "I ain't hungry no-how. I'll see you in the bed, woman."

Mattie remained on her hands and knees, babbling to the empty room. A single Bob Howler moth flew erratically around the bare light outside on the porch, its huge body thudding dully against the bulb.

⚭⚭

Putting Away Childish Things

Whitey Roy mopped sweat from his forehead with a gear oil-stained red bandana. Everybody knew that the ancient gas pump at Dunnavant's service station ran slower as the temperature climbed. Though the faded printing on the oversized disk thermometer, nailed crooked to the side of the office door, topped out at 105, its rusty red needle was pinned far beyond that. Whitey figured it was at least 110 degrees.

Across Pigeon Roost Road, Mac Murphy's hay field wavered like smoke, as though the landscape was smoldering in the late afternoon sun. A few dun-colored cattle stood still as statues, except for the occasional fly-swatting swish of a tail. A puff of breeze raised dust on the gas station's buckled pavement. It felt more like an open pizza oven than wind. All the while, the faded numbers on the pump rolled slowly. At this rate, he thought, it'll take an hour to fill this five gallon can.

The pump said: *"Klackity-chuff, squeeek. Klackity-chuff, squeeek. Klackity-chuff, DING."* From the tired sound of the thing, Whitey could definitely tell it was running down. He wanted a cigarette and a beer. If the damn gas nozzle still had the auto-clip on it he would have left it stuck in his battered red gas can and lit one up in the shade of the scraggly hackberry tree at the edge of the parking lot.

Whitey Roy knew he was not the sharpest tool in the shed, but, as he repeated often, "My momma didn't raise no dummy." He could smell the fumes from the 97 octane like he had his face right there in the can. He mopped ineffectively at the sweat running into his eyes and squinted at the hay barely shifting in the blast furnace air. "Ker-poof," he said, imitating the last sound he would likely hear if he lit a match near that pump.

Everything looked burned around the edges; a comic book portrayal of some rural hell where all the colors were washed out. The grinding innards of the pump slowed noticeably. It was too hot to get excited, but Whitey considered it. He could have gone to the Phillips 66 further up 31 at the end of Buford's Station, but that would have taken another half hour and he was already behind in raking his hay. He sighed.

A shadow poured quickly like paint, spilled over the station, plunging him into shade. The relief was overwhelming. Before he could look up at the cloud that caused it, the pump squealed to a halt. The numbers stood frozen at three point three gallons. He clicked the handle twice and looked into the nozzle end, shook the thing a few times, and said, "Aw, c'*mon!*" That's when he felt it.

At first the rumble seemed to be in the air around him. After a moment, he dropped the pump handle and clapped his hands over his ears, but it didn't help much. Charley Spits' beagles started howling and yapping next door. It got darker, and cooler, and the wind rose and threw candy wrappers, empty beer cans, and small stones around the lot in spirals.

"Mus' be a tornada," he murmured.

Something hard smacked him on the shoulder and the vibration in his legs felt like an earthquake. The rumble became a violent shaking.

Whitey bent forward with an unavoidable wave of nausea and projectile vomited his turkey sandwich onto the oil-stained pavement. He fell to his knees, grinding skin into the tar and shredding his jeans. The low frequency pulsing was joined by a piercing high note that descended the tonal scale so rapidly that all the glass in his truck windows, the store front, and the face of the pumps exploded, spraying shards of glass .

The pressure grew inside his head; blood leaked from his ears. He opened his mouth to scream, but the sound was drowned out. A barn-sized disc shot out of the dark above him and descended over the hay field and stopped fifty feet above the small herd who did not seem to notice the commotion.

The rumble and squeal blinked out and the wind died. The resultant silence revealed a quieter purring sound that came from the direction of the disc. Cows lowed, tails swished. Whitey Roy tried to catch his breath. He couldn't.

He was still on his bleeding hands and knees when he realized that the pavement was scorching hot. Jumping to his feet, he wiped at his runny nose and eyes with the sleeve of his dirty denim shirt. He tried to focus on the disc hovering above the cattle. It was at least two hundred feet across. The surface was dull, dark gray, like primer paint. There was no texture or marking on its smoothness.

Whitey wanted to run, but his legs refused to obey. He fought the urge to vomit and defecate simultaneously. The part of his mind that usually held a running commentary about things was mute, struck dumb by the enormity of the thing. His heart felt like a clogged drain. Not enough blood was getting to his head.

As though a vacuum cleaner were switched on, two of the four or five cows flew up into the sky disappearing into the bottom of the disk. One more followed, tumbling head over hind and mooing once just before vanishing. The last two evaporated similarly.

Whitey mumbled, "Cows..."

Without a sound, the disk swooped off at a forty-five degree angle and paused like a hummingbird several miles away. He looked up into the darkness and realized that the clouds he thought had covered the sun actually looked like the reflection of a city in the surface of a river. The disc shot into an opening in the face of this upside-down city. After a moment it began to move away slowly, growing smaller as it receded, the low rumbling was much quieter but still present. Soon it had become small enough for the afternoon sun to shine under it, illuminating the sides of buildings and the sparkling glass of a hundred million windows. Within a minute, it shrunk to a dark smudge in the sky's bright blue field.

Whitey stood in the glaring sun, mouth agape, for a second. The pump began to gush gasoline, soaking his boots, cuffs and calves. He reached out toward the handle, but before he got it, the pump rang one final time and the flow ceased. The wind picked up again, slightly cooler now, though the sun was just as searing as it had been moments before the darkness approached.

Whitey shivered. His mind was as blank as a flat rock. A scrap of lined notebook paper blew against his chest and stuck there like it was glued to his shirt with paper hanger's paste. He pealed the sheet off and looked at its surface. It was a brightly colored crayon drawing done by an unsteady child. The picture clearly showed a pink, four fingered hand reaching down toward five tan cows in a field of tall green grass. Whitey Roy's arm dropped to his side, fingers relaxing. The wind snatched the page away. It shrank to a speck, finally disappearing into Mac Murphy's field.

❧❧

That Smell Just Before Rain

Cassia Bernard was replaying the conversation in her mind for the third time as she picked her way through the crowded sidewalk. The suited hoards shuffled toward their evening commutes.

In the memory she whined, "But Mrs. *Shoop*, I just don't get it. I follow the rules and I *still* get the wrong answer."

And Mrs. Shoop replied, "Whatever you do to one side of the equation you must do to the other side, Cassia. That's what the equal sign means."

"Tisk, this is the end of my *life*, Mrs. Shoop. Can't you just give me a B? I promise I will make it up to you." If it were Mr. Nagle, the biology teacher, he'd have done it. Cassia knew the male teachers reacted to her short shorts and low cut camisoles, though she didn't think about why.

Mrs. Shoop responded, sliding her glasses up off the tip of her nose. "Ms. Bernard, that's not how I run my classroom. Do the work and you'll get the grade."

Bitch, Cassia fumed. *I wish I could turn her into the bug she looks like and squash her with my heel!*

The Shoop and her oversized thick eyeglasses were ruining Cassia's 4.0 average. *Math! I can't help it if theorems and equations are boring!* She tossed her empty milkshake cup on the street as she stepped off the curb between two parked cars.

Wayne Carlton had been in Nashville, Tennessee for only two days. He would have to wait two more to return to Bayonne, New Jersey and it was two days too long. "Why don't you go back to Bum Fuck, you flaming ass-wipe?" he screamed as he flipped the other driver the bird, continuing, "Gaddammit ta hell," and spraying spittle on the inside of his driver's side window. Tires squealed as he cranked the steering wheel to the right and bounced up over the cement curb of the I-65 entrance ramp. A hubcap spun away as he floored the rented Impala back on to the road in front of the "ass-wipe," fish-tailing the car wildly.

Carlton continued ranting at the empty interior of his car, absently wiping his runny nose. "It just goes from bad to worse. I can't believe they lost the fucking package. I mean, what the fuck, man? How can you lose something like *that*?" Coming out of Wayne's mouth it sounded like "dat." "And this mutha-fuckin' traffic! Why in the hell do they even let these fuckin' back-woods nigger cunts drive in the first place?"

After about 400 feet the flow of cars simply stopped. He leaned on the horn for a solid second and then banged the dashboard with the palm of his hand.

"Fuckit. Who gives a whore's infected ass if this is a non-smoking car." He groped around in the vest pocket of his jacket and shook out a Pall Mall. Glancing at the dashboard he muttered, "Shit. No fuckin' lighter," and began searching in his pants pocket.

Cars passed him on the right shoulder. Without looking, Wayne sped into the line, holding up the "fuck-you" finger to the blaring horn honking behind him. The forgotten cigarette dangled from his mouth. The trail of vehicles exited about a half mile up the highway. Wayne found himself on Broadway, bumper to bumper, facing downtown. "Mutha fucker, where in the land of sweet fucking Jesus am I now?"

⁓

Cassia hardly noticed the traffic. She was looking across the broad street into the crowd on the other side. Her best friend, Sala, was working as a waitress in the pizza joint next to Two Doors Down. Cassia hoped to catch her when her shift ended so she could hitch a ride home.

The steady stream of cars on the six lane boulevard crept along, lurching to a stop as the north-south lights cycled from green to red. There was little risk of getting run over on this road at this hour, since you could literally walk up to drivers and knock on their windows.

Cassia made her way between the stopped cars weaving diagonally across the road toward the Fourth Avenue crosswalk. When the light changed she was in the middle of the street. By the time she crossed the left-turn lane, the light had turned red, and traffic was once again at a standstill. As she walked between two rows of cars, the driver to her right reached out of his window and patted her ass.

"Hey buddy! What's your problem?" she shouted, smiling and winking as she scooted out of reach. She skirted the curb on the corner and walked into the crosswalk across Fourth just as the Broadway light changed.

⁓

The damn light was taking forever. With the Pall Mall still dangling from his bottom lip, Wayne had resorted to emptying the glove box and console compartment, throwing papers on the floor, searching for a match or a lighter. The driver of a cement truck behind him leaned on his air horn while Wayne was slouched across the passenger seat. He jumped, hitting his head on the roof.

"Fuck me!" He yelled, "You rat bastard," and floored the Impala into the nearly empty block ahead. The next light, at Fourth Avenue, had already turned yellow, and Wayne knew he couldn't stop fast enough to avoid slamming into the stalled wall of traffic beyond it. He cranked the wheel left in an illegal turn while flipping the bird to the cement truck driver in his rear view. By the time he looked down Cassia Bernard was directly in front of the driver's side of his car, and he was traveling at least sixty miles per hour.

Wayne Carlton cut the wheel right and tried to slam on the brakes with both feet, but he was seconds too late. The right front of his rented car became buried in the grill of a ten wheel Mack dump truck. The full force of his acceleration ended instantly when the Impala met six tons of stationary iron. Wayne was catapulted through the windshield onto the street, where his limp body crumpled and somersaulted into the orange brick corner of the African Imports shop. His cigarette was still firmly clenched in his teeth as he lay supine, hands twitching. His brains puddled out onto the concrete next to his split open skull.

Cassia stood frozen amid the hot noisy chaos. Sirens were already approaching. A woman in an ankle length mink coat and three-inch fire engine red heels grabbed her by the shoulders and breathlessly asked, "Are you okay honey?" She smelled of cheap vodka and wintergreen Altoids. "You just about met your *Maker*, darling!" Cassia realized that she was not breathing and ventured a hitching inhale. Glancing down the crosswalk at Wayne's spasming right hand, she vomited her entire milkshake and French fries onto the front of the mink and abruptly collapsed to the pavement in a heap.

"He could have run me over," Cassia said. She was sitting on the edge of her bed, alternately touching up fuchsia polish on her toes and peering out of her second story bedroom window, talking on the phone to Sala. "I could be dead." Some neighbor's dog was barking, rhythmically, a few streets over. Cassia thought. I wonder if that dog ever stops to breathe, or eat, or drink...

"I don't know what you're worried about girl. It's better him than you." Sala's voice was punctuated by pots clanging in the background. "He died because it was God's will, and you didn't for the same reason. Besides, I heard his head was split open like a ripe melon."

"I don't really remember, isn't that weird?" Cassia replied, frowning. "Maybe...you know, he didn't run me over, but he should have. I mean..." She noticed a large orange tabby cat outside in the yard stalking a sparrow nesting in a low branch of her mom's forsythia bush. As she watched, the cat leaped into the air and swiped at the bird, narrowly missing as the sparrow launched. "I don't know," she continued as the cat stalked away, tail twitching. "I can't seem to say exactly what I mean. It's like he died instead of me."

"Cassia," Sala began, "you're scaring me, girl. It's like, I don't know what you are even talking about anymore." There was a pause and then Sala's mouth was close to the phone. "You know Pete Monroe from Schecter's U.S. History class has the hots for you and he's so *buff*, and you haven't even told me what color your prom gown is gonna be. I mean, it's *Junior Prom*, girl. What's the matter with you?"

"Maybe it's karma."

"What?"

"You know. Maybe he used up some of my karma, and now I have to pay it back—like a karmic debt or something."

"Are you high, Cassia?"

"No Sala, listen. I was reading this book called, *Born Again to Love* and they were talking about how your karma makes you attracted to people that you were in love with in a past life and..."

"That Satan's lies, Cassia. All Christians know that we go to heaven when we die..."

There was a loud crash and the tinkle of shattering glass on the other end of the phone. Sala said, "Gotta go," and the line went dead.

Cassia sighed. "He used my karma," she repeated. The dog in the distance continued to bark.

"Cassia? Cassia Bernard! If you want to pass this class you had better pay attention, young lady." Mrs. Shoop stood at the front of the math lab, eraser in hand, snapping her fingers at Cassia.

"Oh, sorry, Mrs. Shoop, what was the question?"

The bell rang. Mrs. Shoop said, "See you all next week, and don't forget to study for that quiz on Monday. Cassia, please stay and talk with me for a moment after everyone is gone."

Cassia nodded. Her attention was drawn by a branch scraping on the window. The wind was picking up, and she suddenly realized it was going to storm. Directly on the heels of that thought, she wondered why she would even care, but then she was distracted again by the scraping branch and thoughts of dark clouds and violent weather. She thought, I just can't keep my mind focused on anything!

The other kids filed out of the room, and the door swung shut. Cassia said, "You wanted to talk to me?"

Mrs. Shoop sat on the desk next to her. "Cassia, I know that you had a bad scare the other day. Is there anything you want to talk about?"

Cassia thought she heard thunder in the distance. She blinked once to clear the thought and said, "I don't know where to start." She never trusted Shoop before; maybe this was some sort of a trick. Lightning glowed along the tree line at the far edge of the football field. She realized there *would* be a storm. I wonder how I knew that, she thought.

Shoop broke the silence; Cassia had turned her head again and was searching the darkening sky through the classroom windows. "You seem distracted. Do you want to tell me what happened?"

Cassia turned to her and said, "That man. He died. But it could have been me. He was coming right for me...turned, and then he died. It could have been me..." Her voice trailed off.

Mrs. Shoop kneeled on the classroom floor and put her arms around the girl, pulling her into a tight embrace. "Oh, you poor girl, you poor thing. It's okay, hon. You're okay."

Cassia thought, yes, it is definitely going to rain, and pushed her teacher away with both hands. She looked into Mrs. Shoop's thick glasses; they distorted her eyes. "No," she said. "I am not a poor girl. You're not listening." Thunder rolled outside, low and long. The glass in the windows rattled. "He died, and I didn't. Like one of your equations. What happens on one side has to happen on the other. I was in the way, and the car was moving too fast to stop."

The algebra teacher understood Cassia's words—after all, they were simple English—but she couldn't understand what the girl was trying to say. Lightning flashed again on the other side of the low hills in the distance. Thunder followed. Without another word, Cassia stood up and pushed through the door, leaving Mrs. Shoop kneeling on her classroom floor before an empty desk.

≈

The blood had been cleaned away. The rain had not begun yet, though the wind was whipping trash down the gutter of Broadway. Cassia stood at the corner of Fourth, looking down at the sidewalk where Wayne Carlton's brains had spilled out. There was no sign left of his death. The sea of people flowing around her on the sidewalk took no notice. She was only partly aware of them. She was thinking, if you must perform the same functions on both sides of the equal sign, then this act was unbalanced. She turned and looked at the intersection. Cars were lined up like blood cells in arteries and veins. Green light go: The cells flowed through the valves of the intersection. Red light stop: And other cells flowed in opposite directions. It was like a dance pulsing to an unheard heartbeat.

The first drops of cold rain dotted the sidewalk. The smell of wet pavement twisted off the road like smoke. There's a name for that, she thought. Petrichor, she'd read about it somewhere. Green light: The traffic flowed before her. Red light: One line stopped, one line continued. Dazed, Cassia stepped off the curb and began slowly crossing Fourth Avenue. Thunder rumbled. The rain suddenly swept in like a wave. She stopped in the middle of the street and, eyes closed, raised her face to the deluge. Horns blared, tires slid on wet macadam. She leaned into the sound. It would be alright now, balanced, equal.

The Federal Express truck skidded to a stop a mere inch from Cassia Bernard's soaked blouse. She continued to stand, eyes closed, face upturned to the streaming rain. The red-faced driver jumped down from his cab, his hands balled into fists. He looked as though he was going to bludgeon the high school girl to death right there in the middle of the intersection. He screamed in her face, "What are you? A fucking retard? What the fuck are you doing in the fucking street? I almost ran you over. Are you trying to ruin my life?

❧❧

Marsha Griggs

Asher Todd needed coffee. Actually, he needed ten hours of oblivion in a dark room between cool cotton sheets. He did not need two more hours in a florescent lit surrealist painting. But coffee would do for now. Dr. Todd was at the end of a double shift, what he and the other interns at Vanderbilt Medical Center called *a Brain Crusher*, as in "Hey Ash, can you walk Rufus for me? I've got *a Brain Crusher* tonight." Asher didn't own a dog and he couldn't understand why any intern would, though Rod Burbank asked him to walk Rufus occasionally. "Man," Rod told him over a couple of pints at Dan McGinnis, "Rufus can only hold it for twelve hours, after that he shits all over my fucking bed. Do you think he's trying to tell me something?" Ash thought about telling Rod to get a lower maintenance pet, something like a goldfish or a parakeet, but he kept these critical thoughts to himself. Interns in their last year needed all the support they could get.

Tonight's was the *Brain Crusher* to beat all. The ER seemed less like a hospital and more like a sterile circus, packed from eight PM, when the Predator's game let out, until after two AM when the bars closed down. Armed robberies, car accidents, fist fights, just plain falling down drunk and one head trauma: Marsha Griggs, 42 Calliope Lane, Nashville TN 37216. Unconscious. Prognosis? Ash didn't think she'd live through the night. There was nothing you could do but wait in cases like this, and Dr. Todd did not think they would be waiting long.

Asher asked the ER nurse, Cat Sylvan, "Hey babe, have a look through her purse, won't you?" She eye rolled and side glanced him before striding away muttering. He stood alone for a few moments replaying the fight he and Cat had that morning over breakfast. Why would it upset her so much that he brought her bagel with butter instead of cream cheese? Cat confused him, and Asher Todd was not used to being confused. To divert his mind from the decaying relationship, he surveyed the woman on the table. Her chest rose and fell regularly with the cycle of the respirator. The florescent bank hummed, and the heart/blood pressure monitor beeped. The lights gave her skin a greenish cast. Dr. Todd shuddered.

Marsha Griggs traveled light. She'd been wearing a tan skirt and a blue waistcoat with a white silk blouse, a powder blue "Body by Victoria" bra and a matching color thong. Her legs were shaved but she wore no hose and a pair of blue Kenneth Cole pumps.

At least the silk shirt *was* white and the bra *was* powder blue. These articles were now soaked in Marsha Griggs' type O-negative blood (*same type as mine,* a semi-aware part of Dr. Todd's brain noted), and stuffed into the yellow bio hazard bag, having been cut from Masha's slight body by nurse Sylvan's merciless bandage shears. The bag would soon be tied and hauled to the basement and incinerated, all traces turned a fine grey ash.

Ms. Griggs' heart rate increased to one hundred and ten beats per minute. Her blood pressure touched ninety over one sixty and continued to fall. Her skin was cool and pale. Asher's diagnosis was an intracerebral hemorrhage from a fall or a blunt object blow. Basically, the back of her head was skull split. Blood had leaked from her ears, but since stopped. Her pupils were dark dots extending to the sclera and unchanged by penlight. There were some scrapes on the backs of her shoulders in addition to a jagged wound on her neck beneath the left ear.

Ash lifted the sheet covering Marsha Griggs' body to have a private viewing of her small, naked nipples, but his attention was hooked away by bruises just beneath her shoulders. Someone had pushed her forcefully. The marks were developing the signature violet of recently broken blood vessels. If she lived, which was doubtful, the subdural hematomas would mature to a deep purple highlighted by a lovely jaundiced yellow. He realized that her eventual death would be ruled suspicious. "Probably murder," he said. The word hung in the disinfectant scented air.

The meat wagon had picked her up from an alley by the bus station. Ash said, "Ms. Griggs, you don't look like the sort of girl who rides the Greyhounds or hangs around the mission."

He compressed the tip of her right index finger and watched the capillaries sluggishly refill – a sure sign of blood loss and diminishing vitals. Asher held her small, cool hand for a moment and sighed. After the respirator and the IVs there was really nothing more he could do for her.

The Music City homeless shelter was next door to the bus station. The one-way street, which ran toward the river, was punctuated by strip clubs and bars. The EMT said there were no witnesses and they almost wrote her off as a Jane Doe. He spotted her Calvin Klein purse twenty feet away just as they were loading her in. Asher sensed some sort of unusual puzzle, but he did not have enough brain juice left to assemble the jigsaw.

He estimated that she was about five foot six, one hundred and five pounds. "A little thin for my tastes," he said to nurse Sylvan when came back in. Cat snorted and shoved the blood work report at him. The sheaf of papers splashed across the tiles.

The Griggs woman had small features and olive-colored skin. Asher's old undergraduate roommate would have called her "Elvin," but that was only because Sam had a penchant for all things *Lord of the Rings*; her ears did seem slightly pointy though.

Cat told Asher, "Look doctor, you can rummage through this girl's personal effects yourself. I don't have time for your shit." She spun to exit and postscripted: "You're an asshole, Asher." He thought, the makeup sex would be great, babe, if you can just let go of it. But at hour fourteen of this sixteen hour *Brain Crusher,* he could not even attempt to articulate the sentiment. *I'll have to take some time to apologize later, maybe get some flowers at the gift shop.* His thoughts were sluggish and disconnected. Ash folded his glasses into his shirt breast pocket and rubbed both eyes with his palm heels.

After tossing the report aside, he dumped the contents of Marsha Griggs' tan clutch purse onto the stainless steel counter. The small pile rattled loudly. He used a plastic Bic pen to push the items around, not because he was concerned about contaminating himself, but because he was exhausted and cross-eyed and the activity gave him some perverse, if not fully recognized, pleasure.

There was a Tennessee driver's license with a blank organ donor section, a blue DKNY compact, a yellow Universal pencil (made in China) with a broken tip and a white number ten business sized envelope.

No wallet, no keys, no cell.

The envelope had something scrawled on it in a smudgy script. It was almost illegible. Asher considered calling Metro, but they were sure to be poking around plenty later. There would be an autopsy for sure, though the cause of death looked pretty obvious. "Zee human person can't-a live too long with a completely smashed scull und 35% blood loss," he said aloud in a strange foreign accent. His voice made a metallic echo in the tile and stainless room. God I'm so tired I'm beginning to babble, he thought. He held the envelope up to the pulsing florescent lights and shook the contents, but could not see through the safety paper. It contained a hard nugget of an object, about an inch long, a quarter inch thick. Asher pressed the paper down around the item and felt its lumpy outline. It was a key—from a storage locker.

He squinted at the writing on the front. He could almost make out a name: Albert or Alfred. The first letter of the last name was either T or Q. It was no use. If this were written by Ms. Griggs' dainty hands he would have been surprised. Someone else had scribbled these hieroglyphics and given it to Marsha. Or maybe she stole it...

Asher's imagination ran on its own track now, like he was watching a late night TV mystery. The Southern Ohio freight whistle blew breathy and faint from the yard adjacent to the college along the Cumberland River. An overhead page smacked him into the present.

"Dr. Todd to the ER desk, Dr. Todd..."

"Shit," Asher said to no one. *I guess this night isn't over yet.* He used the side of his palm to sweep the contents back into the purse, but the envelope missed the small opening and fell with a muffled clink.

Asher stared at the white rectangle and pictured the lockers at the Nashville Greyhound station. He had never seen them, but he was sure they were there. The overhead paged him again:

"Dr. Todd...STAT."

"Alright already," he mumbled to the garishly lit room. "Hold your fucking polo ponies." In his sleep deprived state, Asher Todd had become infected by an irrational desire to check the lockers. It tugged at him like the smell of sex.

He plucked the envelope from the floor, and stuffed it into his exam coat instead of putting it in the purse. Asher dreamed of dancing locker keys and seedy singing mission-district prostitutes dressed as 1940s nurses in white vinyl, but he forgot the dreams upon waking thirty-two hours later. By that time Marsha Griggs had given up the sheet that replaced her Liz Claiborne skirt and J. Jill silk shirt. In its place she wore a manila colored tag on her right big toe and her body temperature was down to a brisk forty three degrees Fahrenheit. Most of the blood had been washed off of her face, but there was still a considerable amount of it matted and drying in her short blond hair. Though the nail beds of her fingers were cyanotic blue and the block beneath her neck created a disturbing wrinkle behind the ears—ears Asher Todd thought were pointy and kind of cute—anyone would think that Marsha Griggs had been an attractive woman. But they would have been wrong. She wasn't a woman at all.

Asher woke in the half light of dusk. It was 8:30 PM. The inside of his mouth felt as though he'd been chewing on kitty litter. He was afraid of what his breath might smell like. After standing for what seemed like fifteen minutes in front of the toilet, his bladder finally emptied, and he shuffled off to the inadequate kitchen of his efficiency hole-in-the-wall to seek coffee.

Asher's refrigerator was empty aside from a quart of organic whole milk, a jar of Clawson pickles and a white Styrofoam take out box, the mystery contents of which would not be solved this evening. There was little to eat or drink in his cabinets. What Dr. Todd's kitchen did sport was a professional Mazzer burr grinder and a top of the line Ranchillio one group head espresso machine, complete with a professional steaming wand.

The young doctor would introduce women to his coffee maker by the name Georgiana. To the introduction he would predictably add, "Life is just too short to drink bad coffee." He had not yet graduated to roasting his own, but that day would come. Nashville wasn't exactly a coffee wasteland, but when he finished his internship he would be making his way to the Pacific Northwest. Seattle or Portland, where, as he would also often say, "Real coffee is king, my friend; the promised land of the caffeinated."

He bumped his exam coat, which fell off the back of a kitchen chair, and the number ten envelope slid out of the pocket. It stopped, wedged half under his refrigerator by the bulge of the key.

Asher had forgotten about Ms. Griggs until that moment. A small shudder began at the base of his spine (lumbar vertebrae six, his well-trained brain chimed in) and slowly, maddeningly clicked up each bone in his back toward his shoulders.

"Those pointy ears..." he mumbled, reaching for the envelope.

While Georgiana warmed up, Asher sat at his tiny table and tried to summon the personal ethics or moral centering that would coerce him to return the envelope. By the time the green light went from blinking to solid he had not succeeded in conjuring any feelings other than intensified curiosity. *This is madness.* He tried to convince himself, but he already had an erection, his body knew it was going to the bus station even if his foggy brain had not yet realized its fate.

He packed the portafilter and expertly compressed the perfectly ground beans to exactly eight pounds, slid a two ounce shot glass beneath the spout while tightening the head in place, and hit the brew switch.

While the creama collected in the crystal glass, Asher Todd tore the envelope open and poured its contents onto his countertop.

The brass key had an orange plastic ring around the shank with the number twenty-six embossed in white. He flipped it over, twisted the valve on the steam and foamed the three percent milk for his latte. *Definitely a locker key, probably from the Greyhound station where Ms. Griggs was discovered.*

Asher's brain caught up to his body. Adrenalin zigzagged though his bloodstream. He sipped his latte imagining the locker's contents: *Money? Papers? Secrets?* Without realizing it, he had committed to finding the locker and opening it, passing over any rational questions. He did not ask himself why; it became his vision of conquest for the evening. As the sky through his west-facing windows quickly cycled through all the shades of grey to night, he drank his coffee picturing a living, breathing Marsha Griggs as though he possessed a key that would open her.

Young Dr. Todd arrived at the mission on Demonbreun Street just after the thin band of light on the horizon finally gave up to dark, dressed in engineer's boots, jeans and a blue chambray shirt. He parked and walked the two short blocks back up the street to the bus station. Even after dark the temperature had to be at least ninety. On the way he handed out all of his pocket change to two grey-skinned weather-beaten men and one legless, toothless woman of indiscriminate age. By the time he reached the bus station his armpits and shirt back were sweat soaked.

His glasses fogged with condensation as he walked through the second set of glass doors into a wall of frigid air-conditioning. He removed them. The lockers were directly across from a bank of broken pay phones just inside the doors.

The shudder at lumbar vertebra number six began scrambling around again like a caged ferret. He crossed the floor dodging an unbelievably thin woman hauling a beat-up suitcase by one hand and two scrawny boys with crew cuts by the other.

The building was crowded and stank of Simple Green disinfectant cleaner and stale tobacco. An overhead speaker announced arrivals and departures in a thick Nashville twang, just as unintelligibly as any other bus station.

Number twenty-six was in the second block of lockers, sixth one down from the top, which positioned it around the level of Asher Todd's chest. He had been fingering the brass key in the right front pocket of his jeans. Metallic brass odor was so strong on his fingers that he could smell it as he brought the key out and slid it into the slot in the grey metal panel.

As he turned the key he thought he could hear the tumblers turn. A deep, suspicious part of his brain objected to this information, *there are no tumblers in a keyed lock...* the thought distracted him from noticing what happened next. He automatically pulled the door open and bent slightly to peer into the darkness. The locker was empty.

Well that's depressing, he thought. Don't know what I thought I was going to find.

He really believed the locker contained some clue to Marsha Griggs' death or maybe a big brown paper bag full of crumpled one hundred dollar bills.

He filled his lungs with air and spun on his heel—plans for the rest of his evening began filling his mind—and began to exhale in a resigned sigh. It caught in his throat.

The cavernous bus station lobby was deserted. He froze, looking slowly around the room, and muttered, "What?" The word echoed. He pressed the heels of his palms into his eyes and shook his head slightly to clear his fog filled brain.

"Hello?"

Echo and silence.

Louder: "Hel-*lo*."

The room went black. Red terror filled Asher's well-disciplined mind. An icy ripple rolled across his scalp as he struggled to control his muscles. Irrationally, he turned to close the locker in a grasping hope of returning the world to normal, but immediately rejected it and turned back to the doors.

Faint light from the Nashville night glowed through the glass, guiding him out. He found himself on the sidewalk where the sharp edge of the heat had curled off slightly, and a breeze stirred candy wrappers in the gutter.

Asher's heart was still slamming against his ribs as he looked up and down the deserted moonlit street. He willed his breathing to slow. A slight wind blew across his ears. The normal commotion of the city was absent leaving only this alien ear rustle and the ambient background whistle of his own brain.

Twenty-eight-year old Dr. Asher Todd, a young man who had sailed purposefully through his undergraduate and medical schooling with no physical or mental hesitation, stood in front of the Nashville Greyhound bus station with his mouth open trying to comprehend what had happened. He could not. It was as though his mind had gone through a reset. His thoughts were repeatedly derailed by fragmented images of the past few days.

I took the key, I came to the station, I opened a locker...

As soon as he realized that he was still standing alone in what appeared to be a completely empty world, his well-organized brain would begin to replay the details again, like a toy train on a small circular track. The image of a red and silver plastic Lionel Santa Fe locomotive took over his imaginings, complete with the scratchy electric train sound.

When she put her hand on his shoulder from behind, he nearly pissed his pants. "Excuse me," she said.

Asher's mouth was still open when he spun to her. Though she was shorter, they were nearly touching noses.

"Excuse me," she repeated.

He recognized the barely contained terror in her eyes mirroring the confusion of his own mind. Automatically, his arms encircled her trembling shoulders and they embraced. She pressed her slight body into him and grasped him tightly; her head turned toward his neck and rested in the hollow of his shoulder. She sobbed.

They stood that way for a few moments. He thought, holding on to her feels good, right. He began to think coherently. He stroked her back watching over her shoulder as his large hand slid across the blue material of her suit jacket. He breathed in a long draft, smelled her perfume and a slight undercurrent of something else not un-pleasant but incongruent. It was a familiar smell, but one which did not belong: faintly animal and wild.

The woman broke away and gazed up into his eyes. She said, "We have to go. We can't stay here."

The statement didn't leave a space for discussion. Asher realized that she was right, though the itch of a thought (somehow connected with that smell) teased his mind. Maybe because of the inexplicable disappearance of all people, or the relief of locating another human so soon after the terror of total darkness, he instinctively knew they must flee.

They walked briskly toward his car. Three long strides along she stopped and turned, pointing back at her purse on the sidewalk.

"Would you get my bag, Ash?"

He was bending down for it when he realized she had called him by name. As he stood up, the tan clutch was in his hand, and he saw the Calvin Klein logo. He opened his mouth.

The force of impact was tremendous and bone crushing. Asher had a moment to see the woman in the blue suit jacket and matching pumps spring the fifteen or so feet over the sidewalk toward him. She transformed in mid leap.

What Asher saw was a blur. If he had time to reflect (which he did not) he would have seen the slight, attractive, business clad young woman streak toward him in the dim moonlight, her form rearranging impossibly as she shot forward. The transformation looked like a reflection in the surface of water when a large stone is thrown. The complete picture splintered into ripples, and the fragmented reflections re-assembled themselves into a solid image again, but the form that she became was not at all the form she had been.

What Asher saw in the brief moments before she hit him was her narrow head followed by an elongated black body covered with oily, fluttering scales. Her tiny ultraviolet pin prick eyes lasered him from a nose-less face predominated by a wide grin filled with several rows of glinting, needle-teeth.

She slammed him into the brick wall crushing his skull. She cradled his limp body in her webbed palms, wrapping long frog-like legs around his hips. Her amphibious crotch created sticky suction against the taut skin of his belly. The needles of her teeth sliced into his rippling carotid artery. She hummed and trembled as she sucked.

Forcing herself to stop, she tore away from his neck, stood and dropped his body to the concrete. She fingered his face gently, almost lovingly, as she spoke. It sounded to Asher like his own voice garbled and underwater.

"I thank you Asher Todd," she paused and cleaned the blood from her teeth with a flick of her reptilian tongue, "Good of you to attend my invitation." Asher felt a violent wave roll through his broken body. When it subsided, he could see that his legs had morphed;

they were naked now, thinner and shaved, feet ending in a pair of blue Kenneth Cole pumps. His thoughts were woozy, blurred and filled with buzzing, flashbulb spots of random colors. His mouth opened and closed soundlessly.

The jaundiced sodium vapor street lights above the sidewalk blinkered on one by one as she stood. Her alien body had transformed into a young man wearing black leather boots, jeans and a blue chambray shirt. He dropped a brass key into a white number ten envelope, and scribbled something on it before licking the glue and sealing it. The tongue was unnaturally long, thin and the color of a bruised plum. As the young man bent and stuffed the envelope into her tan clutch purse he looked over at Asher's crumpled body and winked.

The last thought Asher Todd had before he lost consciousness was: *Marsha Griggs.*

Abraham's Absolution

"I jus' *has* to save a life, Miss Karen," Abraham said, trembling. Sweat seeped into the collar of his starched shirt, buttoned tight against his Adam's apple. "Lawd knows, Miss Karen, I jus' *has* to!"

Karen Winton, a volunteer CPR instructor recently relocated to Columbia, Tennessee, didn't know which was more inappropriate: The ancient, exhausted, dark chocolate-colored man kneeling in his frayed black suit, or being calling Miss Karen.

"Mister Broom," Karen said, "You don't have to call me Miss..." but it was no use. Abraham had begun again, hands clasped, pumping into the elastic chest of the CPR dummy and counting: "One, two, three..."

Karen slipped into to a cheerleading mode, "Make sure you use your weight and not your muscles, that's right, thirty pumps and two assist breaths. You're doing great..."

But the tall man, folded impossibly on the floor next to the Red Cross dummy, only reached twelve before he collapsed panting. He looked to Karen, his forehead resting on the mannequin's cloth-covered arm, as if he might be sobbing, but he was just catching his breath.

"Mister Broom." Karen said the name louder than she intended and the rest of the class looked up at her. She blushed and covered a tiny moth-hole on Abraham's worn shoulder pad with her hand.

"Mister Broom, let's take a little break, okay? Come over here and have a drink."

Both of Broom's knees snapped as he struggled to stand. They walked to the edge of the room and Karen offered a Dixie cup from the cooler. The dark man wrapped his long fingers around the paper cup and drank slowly, his eyes closed. When he finished he looked directly into Karen's eyes and said, "Thank you kind, Miss Karen." A broad smile spread across his face revealing perfect white teeth. Karen began, "Mister Broom...," but Abraham raised his hand and said slowly, "As a young'un I was taught respect, Miss Karen. Them's old habits and old habits don't never die."

"But you have to tell me why it's so important to learn CPR at your age. I mean, meaning no disrespect, but wouldn't it have done you more good as a younger man?"

"Well that may be so, may be so," Broom's eyes lost focus. He stared at nothing for a moment and then back at her. "Miss Karen, is there someplace we could go and talk?"

Karen invited him to sit in one of the padded chairs in the office. She sat in the other. Abraham peered into the dark well of his long life, waiting for his eyes to adjust. He waited so long that Karen began to worry he was sleeping with his eyes open. Karen opened her mouth and Broom began.

"My daddy was born in Clayton, Mississippi in 1860. I was born in Athens, Alabama in 1905 when he was 40. My momma was 25 but she didn't live long after I came along. She left me and my four brothers and two sisters for my daddy to raise. He died when I was fifteen. Our family lived in a one-room cabin near the Tennessee River. It was small, but clean. As good-a life as we could 'spect, I guess. Grew a little corn, fished the river, made our way as best we could. My brothers had itchy feet. So when they was old 'nuf, they went they north like most black folk.

"They went straight north, ya hear?

"If you lived in South Carolina you'd go to New York. But us folk in Alabama went to Chicago. That's jus' the way we was taught. My daddy learned from his daddy and I learned from him. Don't go east. Don't go west. Taught me to follow the stars and go straight north. My sisters married local and had babies. By the time I stopped growing I was alone in that cabin. I kept the corn up, chopped wood, whatever I could do. 'Fore long I married Della and we began havin' babies too. I never really wanted to go too far from my home."

Karen watched the man making his carefully measured speech. The suit, which probably fit him well twenty years before, was now easily two sizes too large. His pants billowed around his stick-thin legs and his boney wrists stuck out of the jacket sleeves giving him a scarecrow appearance. The sweat had dried from his forehead leaving his skin with a waxy shine. Karen did the math. If Broom was born in 1912 that would make him 102. She had figured the man was in his eighties or nineties. She thought, this guy is a walking relic!

Karen imagined his long life stretching back before she was conceived, trying to picture Abraham Broom's brothers and sisters. A big family, she thought. She was an only child. And here in this small southern town she was an anonymous soul who lived alone in a studio apartment two blocks from the Red Cross office. She worked days at the nearby Saturn plant in Spring Hill, and though there were professional relationships in her life, she kept to herself. She was never quick to make friends and now as a middle aged woman, she claimed she preferred her solitude.

He resumed abruptly, shocking Karen. "There was moonshiners in Parley's woods back then. Hell, I 'spose there's moonshiners there even today. But back then, them Reese boys didn't cotton to none of us black folks. Called us nigras, they did. Ignorant sons of bitches."

He looked up at her, "'Scuse my language, Miss Karen. I have forgotten myself. Now where was I?"

Before Karen could answer he continued, "I've known me plenty of white folk. Mistah Sneed, the man who owned my cabin—he was a fine man. But them Reese boys was nothing but trash. They spent most nights makin' that corn mash and most days drinking it. They was ugly-mean. That's all there was to it.

"When my daughter Sarah was born she was a sickly child. Her lungs didn't work right. She always had the croup. And one day my Della calls me in from chopping and tells me that little Sarah has stopped her crying, and that's a bad sign, Miss Karen. That signals the little one's strength has done give out. And Della, she tells me to go fetch the doctor. Normally I would take a wide detour around Parley's. I never had no truck with them Reese boys. But Della say 'you hurry. Run, Abraham! I don't think she's gonna last and so I runs by the river, and I tries to be quiet.

"Mathew Reese, the oldest of the three, saw me and called for his brothers, Samuel and Robert. They was big boys. They ran me down and held my face in the water. Nearly drowned me. Then they dragged me and tied my wrists up to a big twisted sugar maple limb.

"I still remember it to this day. I was soaked to the skin and the flies was buzzin' round our heads. Matt, he says 'What the hell you think you doin' nigra?'

"I was scared. I was worried about my little Sarah and I tried to tell them boys, but they just laughed and said they didn't give a damn about no black dog's child. Matt and his brothers were piss yoself drunk. They had willow switches and my shirt was tore off."

Abraham rose from his seat and let his jacket slip from his shoulders. With his skinny, long, trembling fingers he slowly unbuttoned his shirt and cuffs. Karen's neck and face flushed. She thought briefly about how bad it looked for a student to be stripping down in

93

a closed office. Instantly the thought was replaced by the realization that this man was old enough to be her grandfather. In an impossibly deft movement Abraham peeled the shirt from his shoulders and let it hang from his waist. His back was covered with a Jackson Pollack of crisscrossed thick and thin pink scars reaching from his shoulder blades extending into the waistband of his black trousers. Karen struggled to think of something to say, but the image blanked her mind.

Broom had turned away from her. She sat unable to move. He spoke to the wall but Karen could clearly hear the tremble in his voice. "It's been seventy-seven years and I still cry for my baby girl. I guess a daddy never gets over the death of his daughter." He turned and began re-buttoning his shirt.

"They left me hanging there. I was passed out in the noon sun. It is a wonder to Gawd that I didn't die m'self. There weren't nothing a black man could do about it. I mean, the police woulda done worse. I just buried my little girl and went back to my life. But the injustice of it burned me more than those willow sticks. It jus' ate at my heart and made me mean. Della told me I needed to get right with my Maker. I wasn't sleeping. So I would get up and wander by the river at night.

"Without thinking, I wandered close enough to hear them Reese boys and I watched from a safe distance. Have you ever heard the saying 'mad enough to make my blood boil?' Well, Miss Karen, I was out of my mind, mad with grief and my heart was black and filled with vengeance.

"I couldn't think a nothing else. Next night, I came back to my hiding place but I brought my ax. I hid, hardly breathing by the hole they'd dug as a privy. It stank and the flies was thick, but I waited, still. I didn't see which one came out first and he never saw me. I split his skull open like a ripe melon. Now you would think that the

94

forest at night was a quiet place but that's not quite true. The night sounds are just different from the day sounds but they are there. Crickets and katydids, owls and other night birds. Them boys were already plastered; they couldna heard a thing if I was standing right next to them.

"I picked off another later on his way to have a piss and by the time the third one recognized that his brothers were gone I snuck up behind him and kilt him where he stood calling. The katydids never skipped a beat.

"I buried the bodies in the soft clay by the river along with all my clothes and I kicked over that still and set them woods on fire. By the time I got home the pink of sunrise had streaked the August sky. I never told no one about it. I heard stories, but I pretended ignorance. Them boys weren't no goddamn good anyway and none too sorely missed. Asides, that fire burned up a hundred acres of dry woods that summer. There wasn't nothin' left for evidence. People jus' assumed that they started the fire and burned up in it." He looked at Karen and his bottom lip trembled. He dropped to his knees and put his hands on the arms of her chair.

Abraham's tears had dried in the cool conditioned air. Three quarters of a century and a hundred miles away from his act of retribution he bowed before this white, middle-aged, CPR instructor from Ohio and begged: "You won't turn me in will you, Miss Karen? You know I killed them in cold blood. I couldn't let them live. And now, before I meet my Lord, I must save a life. I jus' has to Miss Karen . I jus' *has* to!"

Karen laid her hand on the ancient man's curly black head and silently granted the only absolution she could.

≪◈≫

This book was typeset in Century Schoolbook
Designed by Ron Heacock for Libros Igni
Proofed by Alison Bailey
Printed by Gorham Printing, Centralia, WA

RON HEACOCK

www.ingramcontent.com/pod-product-compliance
Lightning Source LLC
Chambersburg PA
CBHW060235180626
46813CB00007B/3091